Where Is Mila?

Jurline G. Younge

Kingdom Builders Publications LLC

Where is Mila?

Where Is Mila?

Kingdom Builders Publications, LLC

Printed in the USA

ISBN
978-0-578-48351-1

Library of Congress Control Number
2019937634

Authored by
Jurline G. Younge

Editor
Kingdom Builders Publications
Wanda Brown

Cover Design
ID 58985017 © Tatsiana Shypulia | Dreamstime.com
LoMar Designs

The people and events in this book are imaginary. If there is any resemblance between my characters and real persons, it is entirely coincidental and unintended.

This book belongs to

CONTENTS

DEDICATION

This book is dedicated to
My husband, Hilton
My daughter, Shelly
And my loving grand kids
Michaela and Niko

Where is Mila?

CHAPTER 1

CHAPTER 1

It was a quiet Sunday afternoon. A lazy breeze danced with the little girls, kissing their cheeks and lifting their soft curly hair as they played under the large cherry tree. Rachael watched her daughters from the kitchen window. She adores these twin girls. Their intense childhood laughter brought a smile to her lips.

Memories took her back in time as she propped herself against the kitchen counter and thought of how these girls came into her life a year ago. It started when she met Sam. It was Monday morning and she was late for work at N.E Windermere, a large popular fabric store in Bridgetown. As she looked into the distance, she saw the 7 o'clock passenger bus approaching. She had to get to the stop quick! It was a wet night, last night and she skipped over puddles of rain water as she ran to the bus stop.

Her heart raced and her breath rasped as she neared her stop. She was 28 years old. "I am out of shape," she thought. Suddenly she could not see. What had happened? She came to a sudden stop, her eyes tightly closed. Blink, blink she opened them and to her horror she was drenched with red sandy water. "Oh my God, I don't believe this!" She turned to see what caused her distress, but as she turned the bus was passing her by. She dropped to her knees, she screamed, "Today is not my day!" As she crouched over in total defeat, she heard a sympathetic voice, "Miss, are you ok?" She looked up, looked down, then up again into the kindest eyes she had ever seen. With a voice filled with emotion, she said, "I know I am going to lose my job today because someone drenched me with road water!"

"I am sorry miss, but I did it, I did not see the pothole!" He declared and offered his hand to help her up. She hesitated, analyzing her situation. Should she yell at him? Should she hit him with her pocketbook? Her emotions got the best of her as tears filled her eyes. She took his hand and he helped her up. "My name is Sam Duncan and I am a taxi driver. I could take you home so you can clean up and change then I can take you to work, is that ok?"

"Thank you," she uttered.

As Rachael quickly showered and changed, Sam sat in his taxi and mulled over the morning event. He leaned his head back and closed his eyes. Rachael's upturned tear-stained face sprang into his mind. Something about her stirred a passion in him that laid dormant for many years.

CHAPTER 2

CHAPTER 2

Sam was a single parent of two daughters Camila and Mila. He worked endlessly to make ends meet. Three years ago, he met the one, or so he thought; the attractive Sue Ellen! They fell in love and she gave birth to twin girls. He begged Sue Ellen to marry him, but she never did. After the birth of their children Sue Ellen became restless and withdrawn from the babies. One day he went to work and when he returned Sue Ellen was gone and the children were left with the next-door neighbor. A note was placed on his pillow which read, "Sorry this is not for me, you are not for me, don't look for me." That was the last day he saw Sue Ellen.

As months passed, his neighbor, Mama Lucy, became his rock. She supported him in the care and nurturing of his daughters. She was mom by day, and he was dad by night.

A horn honked, he stirred and opened his eyes.

He took Rachael to work and could not shake the feeling of wanting to be in her company again. He created scenarios to see and talk to her whenever he could. The relationship blossomed into a true, pure love; a love of which he had never felt before. The couple married.

Sam and Rachael settled into a wonderful life with the two beautiful children, Camila and Mila. Energetic personalities, large sparkling eyes and rosy cheeks which made them almost identical except for their complexion. Camila was dark and Mila was fair. The girls were inseparable.

After a few years, the couple purchased an old fixer upper on Beckles Road, in St. Michael, a parish in Barbados. It was an open style gable house, nestled in a cluster of fruit trees. Year round, there was a constant supply of limes, lemons, cherries, golden apples, akees, and breadfruits.

Rachael worked at N.E Windermere, a fabric store in Bridgetown. She was a dedicated worker and loved by the customers. After years of devoted service, she was promoted to supervisor. At first, she felt daunted by the constant bickering and female clashes she endured eight hours each day, compounded by her boss's flirtatious behavior. She tried to find balance by talking to working women with similar occupations. She also learned how to deal with such situations through nightly research of books and articles on workplace management which dealt with contentious behaviors. She did this because she wanted to be the best merchandizing supervisor she could be.

Sam extended his taxi service by adding two more cars. It was now the Duncan Taxi Service. He acquired an adjacent lot next door after old Ms. Joosebury passed away and built a large taxi garage.

Life was good. The Duncans felt blessed. The girls were now 15 years old and were establishing their own areas of educational focus. Camila was drawn to the subject of educational technology, while Mila expressed an affinity for visual arts.

Camila was more of an analytical thinker, giving deeper thoughts into her area of study. She lingered at school later in the afternoons, meeting and discussing techniques and strategies with her teachers and instructors. At night she was always on the computer figuring out formulas or tinkering with old broken mother boards.

Mila had a natural gift of putting her thoughts on canvas. At the age of 15 her work was displayed in the hallways of her school. Her room was filled with piles of canvases, palettes and pints of all forms and colors.

There was an extraordinary quality within this family in which they shared their joy, pain, happiness and sadness. Each was a piece of a remarkable whole!

One Thursday evening, the sun had just dipped behind a nesting of bamboo trees. A faint strum of guitar music floated on the soft afternoon breeze. Mila left for a quick trip to the corner store. She had forgotten to buy milk earlier. She knew how her dad liked his glass of milk before bed. "Mom I am running to the corner store to get dad's milk; I'll be back in two seconds!"

"Ok Mila," Rachael said. Mila walked down the cobble stone pathway, through the opened gates and did not return home!

CHAPTER 3

CHAPTER 3

Morning broke to an unbelievable reality. Pain wrapped itself around this small family leaving them limp from the shock of Mila's disappearance. They were up all night. They traced her steps; they called the police. The village family embraced them with support and concern.

A retired teacher who resides near the grocery store claimed she saw Mila talking to someone in a white, "real fancy," SUV but she turned away from the window to continue her cooking. When she returned to the window there was no sign of Mila or the SUV.

Camila slowly dragged herself into Mila's room. She collapsed on the floor as the fresh pain laid its weight on top of old pain. "Where is my sister she cried," hugging a canvas of an incomplete painting of herself. Sam entered the room and just the very sight of Camila was sheer agony. He threw himself on the floor and hugged his daughter and their bodies convulse with heart wrenching sobs.

Barbados is a small island with a population of 285,000 people. The police were able to canvas the entire island in a couple of days. They scoured the hills, gullies, caves and beaches. Forensic technicians were brought in from neighboring St. Lucia, but what was discovered were her sneaker prints at the very spot where she was seen talking to someone in the white SUV. After days and days of continual searching there was no news or sign of Mila.

Over time, life slowly shrunk back to its normal routine but not for the Duncan family. Rachel was pregnant. She was going to tell her family the same night Mila disappeared. Rachel collapsed at work one day and was rushed to the Barbados Public Hospital. Rachael lost her baby.

CHAPTER 4

CHAPTER 4

Sam Duncan was a resilient man! Past experiences made him so. There were difficult economic times in South America during the 1940's. Individuals were forced to travel from country to country or island to island in search of a better life. Sam's mother, Sofia, originally from Venezuela, came to Guyana and worked on a gypsy caravan as a young girl. After many years she travelled to Barbados where she met Henry Duncan. Sofia was in love, truly in love. She could not believe her luck when this tall quiet gentleman offered to help her find a job as an interpreter because she was bilingual. Sofia learned to speak English during her travels in Guyana. This tall, handsome, guy with sandy brown hair, and amber colored eyes was her man!

Little did she know Henry had a dark side! Sofia lived with Henry as his common law wife. She bore him two sons, Sam and Simon.

After the birth of Sam, her first born, Henry began to exhibit behaviors that concerned Sofia. She tried to overlook his shortcomings and move on, but slowly Henry became a monster. Sofia and her boys began to suffer unspeakable pain at the hands of Henry. She tried to run away but he always found her and brought her and the boys back. You see, Henry was a sergeant in the military, and he had contacts.

Over the years, this beautiful woman became a fading image of what she once was. Fear, pain, and hurt were all she knew. She and her boys were beaten, thrown out of the house, knocked around, and were left many days without food.

One Saturday at the age of 14, Sam joined some village friends to work on a chicken farm a couple of miles from their home. Simon was left at home with his mom and dad.

"It is Saturday, no school," Simon thought. He lingered between his sheets when suddenly his mother screamed. He jackknifed out of bed and ran to the sound of her voice.

What he saw set off a chain of events that would change their lives forever. Sofia was covered in her own blood that oozed from her mouth. Lying on the floor beside her was two of her front teeth. Henry had drifted up against the back window and was shouting at Sofia.
He said, "I hate you, you hag! Leave, and take your two bastards with you! Go!"

Henry snatched Sofia from the floor and threw her against the stove.

Simon was only 12 years old and was always told he was big for his age. Something inside his head snapped at the sight of his mother who was jammed up against the stove with blood everywhere. With a swift movement he snatched a long-blade kitchen knife and plunged it into his father's chest. The attack was so swift and forceful, Henry stumbled backwards and fell through the window to his death.

Simon could not believe what was unfolding in front of him, he panicked. He ran out of the kitchen, down the steps, grabbed his bike, brushing away the tears and calling out for Sam. "Sam, Sam please come, you gotta make this right." His heart raced; tears flowed as he peddled furiously down the driveway.

Simon rode his bike into an oncoming commercial truck filled with landscaping rocks.

Sofia buried Henry and Simon then flew to Venezuela with Sam. Her relatives readily embraced her and helped her pay for counseling for her and Sam.

Years passed, 14 to be exact. Sam returned to Barbados. As he walked along the beach where he and his brother had walked many years ago, his heart swelled with unbearable pain. His eyes welled up with tears. He did not try to hold them back, "just let them flow, just let them flow for you bro," he thought.

The next day he visited his brother's grave. He sat in the same spot for a long time. He was mired down with so much hurt and sadness, he did not realize how late it was. In his heart he told his brother he, Simon, was the reason for his return. He thought, despite all their adversarial challenges of living with their father, he was going to make a positive mark in this life for the Duncan family.

CHAPTER 5

CHAPTER 5

Yes, Sam was resilient! He made another promise to himself despite the outcome of Mila's disappearance, he will be the solace to move his family beyond this point of pain.

Over time, Sam started to give of himself more than ever before. He would show up at N.E Windermere and take his Rachael to lunch. He would buy her flowers or take her shopping. When his job allowed, he would take Camila to school. He'd also surprise her with a new cell phone and other electronic devices she needed. On weekends he planned family outings, like going to the movies, a picnic in the park or quiet time on the beach.

Sam's mother, Sofia, now lived in Miami Florida. Sofia called her son frequently, giving him all the support, she could.

It was almost the end of the school year. Sam made plans for Camila to visit her grandmother over the summer so she could get to know her better. He also made plans for him and Rachael to join her near the end of the summer. Sam was quite aware of his mother's feelings about the island and never pressured his mother to visit them. He knew she needed more time to heal emotionally.

Before Camila left for Miami, the family decided to spend some time at the beach. The three of them made their way down a winding path around a large esplanade to Browns Beach. Rachael had been working overtime and Camila helped her dad at the taxi office. They were tired and just wanted to kick back on the sand. Camila was in the process of spreading her beach towel when she was startled by someone who walked up to her and said, "Hi remember me!"

Camila took a step back as her large eyes carefully surveyed the young white girl. "No!" Camila said shaking her head from side to side.

"It was a few months ago when we met on the American Airline in Miami. You were very upset with your mom," the girl said.

Camila's thoughts raced, "I wonder what she wants, maybe she's been smoking something, but I don't smell any smoke. I am so-r-ry, but..."

Before Camila could complete her sentence, the blond-haired girl with inquisitive eyes said, "I love your tan. Are you sure you don't remember me? I even gave you a bracelet when you started crying."
Just as Camila was about to answer, a couple standing in the distance yelled, "Come on Arella, we have to go." With that, Arella ran off.

Sam and Rachael heard most of the brief exchange between their daughter and the strange girl. Rachael said, "What was that all about?"

Camila said, "I have never seen that girl before." She looked over at her father and his puzzled look sparked a thought that jolted her. Her heart raced. She said excitedly, "dad, are you thinking what I am thinking?"

Sam was just about to twist open his ice cream soda when his hands fell open, dropping the bottle onto the sparkling sand. His words were almost inaudible, "Oh God! She saw Mila!"

Rachael yelled, "What, what did you say Sam?"

Camila looked around and realized their behavior was attracting onlookers. They quickly packed up and set out to find this Arella. They traversed the beach looking under every umbrella and behind every shady tree but no Arella! They went home.

CHAPTER 6

CHAPTER 6

Their journey home was quiet. Everyone was immersed in their own thoughts, grappling with the possibility Sue Ellen had kidnapped Mila, and Mila was alive in Florida!

Upon entering the house Sam walked to the bar and mixed a strong drink of cockspur and coke. He knocked it back in one gulp and mixed another. Rachael headed to the bathroom as she rummaged through her pocketbook looking for her anxiety pills. Camila cleared the dining table, rolled out a large sheet of paper and began to set up a timeline of Mila disappearance.

They were optimistic, but they treaded cautiously. Rachael, after taking her pill, became drowsy and slowly dragged herself to bed. Sam and Camila stayed up late and used the internet to try to track Sue Ellen's whereabouts. They wanted to have tangible leads before they alerted the police.

Sam and Camila tried their best to keep their discussions positive, but in their hearts, there was the nervous fear of what dangers Mila could be in.

They searched the Miami police blotter and all the Miami newspapers, looking for clues. Sam nodded off for a bit. His eyes snapped opened when Camila said, "Dad, you know Mila is a very smart girl, so my biggest question is why hasn't she tried to contact us?"

Sam said, "You are right, Camila, not one phone call, no text message, not even a letter that could shed some light on her whereabouts."

"Well," Camila replied, "we can safely say her phone has not been in use since that night, because the sergeant in charge of her case checks her phone account every day for leads."

"You know what? I will stop by the station and check with Sergeant Rodrick tomorrow and I will let him know about the mysterious blond girl," said Sam.

Sam and Camila retired to bed.

Three uneventful weeks passed!

* * * *

Dressed in jeans, t-shirt and her backpack, Camila stood at the Grantley Adams International Airport with Sam and Rachel. As they waited for Camila's flight, there were butterflies in her stomach, but she would not let her father or Rachael know about this. She flashed them a brave smile and hugged Rachael.

"I got your list of things you want mom. That raspberry lipstick sure looks good on you, I will get you two tubes."

Rachael guided Camila away from Sam's earshot. "You know how I love you and Mila. Please baby, take care of yourself." A tear slipped from Rachael's left eye, she quickly brushed it away. Rachel said,

"Now, you know we are strong girls and we will not get emotional in your father's presence."

"You are so right mom! Dad has been through too much," Camila said.

Suddenly, the sound of the intercom boomed through, "Passengers boarding American Airline 737 will depart at gate 10. Please have your boarding passes and passports ready."

Rachael allowed Sam to accompany Camila to her gate pulling her luggage along. Rachael watched them as they drifted into the crowd. She could not stop wondering how much their body structure were alike; lean physique, long legs and arms with straight shoulders. Sam hugged and kissed Camila and watched her disappear beyond the immigration gate. At this point Rachael walked over to the concession stand and ordered two sodas.

Camila made herself comfortable, as her flight prepared for takeoff. She reclined her seat back a little and nestled into the soft upholstery. As the plane rose amidst the clouds, she looked through the window and wondered if this is how it feels when you are free from burdensome thoughts. She then fingered through a magazine she picked up at the airport. It contained articles on how to use free cell phone trackers, also on how to find someone online. She folded those for further reading. The passenger next to her was a mature woman like Grandma Sofia. Camila smiled and this encouraged an easy conversation about cooking, plants and aerobic dancing. Camila finally drifted into a shallow sleep during her last hour of flight.

Camila cleared immigration and customs in Miami Florida. Awaiting her was her Grandma Sofia. They hugged, exchanged pleasantries then quickly entered a red Buick driven by a Spanish girl who looked to be in her early twenties. Her name was Jane. She mentioned she and Sofia are neighbors and when she heard her granddaughter was coming, she wanted to help, especially since Sofia recently had eye surgery.

Sam and Rachael were very happy to hear Camila had a safe arrival. They went to dinner, came home and spent some quality time together.

CHAPTER 7

CHAPTER 7

There was this natural bond which developed between Jane and Camila. Jane was an elementary school teacher and was happy at the thought of being able to help Camila improve her Spanish.

Grandma Sofia had done well for herself. Upon her return to Venezuela she enrolled in the local college and obtained her LPN license. Immersing herself in school was the best thing she had done for her and Sam. Remembering the cruel days she spent with Henry Duncan sent shivers down her spine. She recalled the countless nights she had to rock Sam to sleep after he woke up screaming from the horrific nightmares. She always knew Sam would return to Barbados because Simon was buried there.

Sofia did not leave Sam to grow up with all the psychological suffering. Oh no! Throughout elementary, middle and high schools, Sam was counseled by specialists. Sofia knew when he left Venezuela, he was ready to face his past, to move on and be ready to live a normal life. Her "niño" turned out to be "muy bueno!"

When the lower social class of Venezuela felt the pressure from president Chaves's harsh political demands, Sofia knew she had to get out, and get out she did! There was a great demand for bilingual nurses in Florida because of the growing Hispanic population. Sofia seized the opportunity to work in America with no regrets.

Sofia was now in her late fifties and was a nursing supervisor at a local hospital in her town. Over the years she blossomed into a beautiful, strong, professional and kind-hearted woman.

She was passionate about flowers and took up flower gardening as a hobby. Camila enjoyed her stories of her unique finds from what she called the DFC (Dead Flowers Club).

Sofia was able to buy a cozy Spanish bungalow at a low cost during the time when the real estate bubble in the United States exploded. Over time, she personalized her home, making it a warm and inviting place.

Looking around, Camila said, "Grandma Sofia, I do love your home, it is splendid!"

"Gracias mi nieta" What are your plans today?"

Before Camila could answer, the phone rang. It was Jane. Camila paused for a second thinking of Jane as her grandmother answered the phone. At that moment, she realized this easy friendship between them was because Jane reminded Camila of her sister Mila. Jane had this unbelievable personality of finding beauty in almost everything, and not wasting a moment to live and love. Camila could just imagine how her students adored her.

The girls and some other friends decided to spend the day at the beach and to check out a house party later. Camila had a lot of fun with her new friends. She felt included in this group of young teachers.

Sam shared his concern over Camila going to a party with strangers, but Rachael was able to put his feelings to rest after she reminded him how strong Camila was and she always has good judgement.

Camila was in a state of euphoria when she stepped into the party. Camila had never been in the company of such beautiful and intelligent young people before. Small groups of party revelers met and greeted each other as they swayed to music and enjoyed delicious food and beverages.

"Come on Camila, let me introduce you to some more bff's," Jane grabbed Camila by the wrist and meandered around small groups down a hallway. They stopped at an alcove to the entrance of the kitchen. Camila thought this was such a beautiful area. A marble-top wet bar lined one side of the space. Above the bar was a collection of different kinds of liquor from around the word. Camila did identify her dad's famous Cockspur.

A flat screen T.V. was neatly placed behind the counter. Rotating pillow-top stools invited anyone to take a seat. Camila sat and crossed her legs as

Jane offered her some fruit punch. Suddenly there was a burst of laughter and Jane sprung up and dashed over to hug some more friends. She looked over at Camila and guided the group to the bar. While Jane introduced Camila to the young men and women, someone yelled, "Hey guys, listen to this!" Jake who was one of the young men from the group had turned on the television. "Did you all hear of that double murder in Coral Gables?"

"What?" said someone behind Camila. All heads turned towards the T.V.

A gasp escaped Camila's lips as the reporter showed pictures of the individuals who were murdered. Camila knew her heart stopped for a second before it started pounding against the walls of her chest. She was riveted to her pillow top stool for a moment. She started to sweat, and she locked her legs tightly to prevent them from wobbling. She looked away, then, looked back at the T.V, staring right back at her were the eyes of her biological mother, Sue Ellen!

"Oh my God!" she said softly.

Camila slowly slipped off her stool and quickly entered the guess bathroom down the hall. Camila was in such a panic. Her thoughts danced wildly in her head. She closed the lid of the commode and sat on it. She wedged her head between her hands. She wanted to scream, cry out, to yank the dispenser from the wall and throw it. She did none of that, instead she mustered control by deep breathing. Her dad taught her that! Slowly she began to regain control of her thoughts.

"I have to get home to Grandma Sofia," she thought. She called her grandma and told her she had a stomachache. Sofia said she was on her way.

Camila found Jane and explained she had to leave because she had a stomachache and Sofia was on her way to pick her up. Jane was very concerned, asking if it might be the fruit punch.

Camila said, "I don't think it was the drink, but I am sure I will feel better tomorrow!"
Jane hugged her new friend and walked with her to await her grandmother's arrival.

The drive took a mere seven minutes throughout which Camila kept the conversation on the delights of the party. Camila allowed her grandmother to eat and take a shower before she broke the news to her.

Sofia was in shock when Camila showed her the pictures and read the details to her from her laptop.

CHAPTER 8

CHAPTER 8

Rays of light streamed through the gaps in the high porous wall of the dark room. Particles of dust danced in the light, grabbing her focus. It was hypnotic! The young girl lay amid the rags on the mangled old cot. As her mind reached back in time, her tears flowed copiously. How she misses her dad and Rachael but most of all Camila! She knew she would do anything on this earth to be with them right now.

She walked back in time thinking how happy she was the evening when she left home to get some milk. It was a beautiful evening! The calypsonian who lived next door was strumming his guitar as he practiced for one of his weekly shows. The sun was saying goodbye for the day as it moved behind the bamboo bushes. As she walked, she thought about the portrait she was painting of her sister. She thought about how much she wanted to capture Camila's serenity.

A white SUV pulled up as she was nearing the store and a friendly woman with a familiar face asked for directions. Mila started to tell her which way to go when the woman flashed her a large smile saying, "I have this GPS, but I need help to set the address, I am not good with technology!"

Mila said, "Oh I can help you with that, my dad taught me how. He has a taxi service."

"Oh thank you sweetie," the woman said as she reached over to open the door. Mila got in! She sensed danger from the moment she heard the locks of the doors click and the vehicle started moving.

"Hey" screamed Mila, "What are you doing?" Before she could grab the steering wheel, a towel with chloroform was shoved into her face. She lost consciousness.

* * *

When Mila regained consciousness, she was aware of what was going on around her, but she never opened her eyes. "Good job Sue Ellen!" a man said.

"Sue Ellen!" Mila thought, "That is my biological mother; the mother who left Camila and me with the neighbor many years ago. Oh no, I don't believe this!"

The voices left the room. Mila opened her eyes her breath, caught in her throat. She could not believe the wealth and grandeur of this room. There were vaulted ceilings meeting high opal colored walls, topped with exquisite valances. A large built-in bed covered with peach and white satin linens dominated the room. This majestic bed was flanked by twin glass night tables. Beautiful teardrop sconces adorned the opposing wall. Slowly her eyes drifted to the large bay window which housed the perfect window seat. Mila slowly sat up as if in a dream. She timidly slid one leg off the bed then the other. She stood, held her breath, thinking at any moment someone would appear. Nothing happened! She moved towards the window, she stopped, she listened then she moved again. Beyond the window were acres and acres of sprawling well-manicured lawns.

Suddenly she sprang into action. "I have to get out of here," she thought. Just beneath the window was a lower extending roof, "I am sure I can get down there and make my escape." She kept her eyes on the bedroom door as she lowered herself through the window. Just as she was about to jump, she heard a scream and words spoken rapidly in Spanish, then more loud talking, her fingers slipped from their grip and she felt herself falling.

A sharp pain seared through her ankle as she landed on the roof. She tried to stop the pain by grabbing her ankle but just as she did, she rolled down the slanted part of the roof. Her screams were filled with fear and pain. She snatched onto something! She opened her tightly closed eyes and realized she was hanging onto a gutter, suspended in the air. She would not look down again because she knew if she did, she would fall to her death. Suddenly there was lots of movement around her and under her. Heads were sticking out from almost every window as four men unfolded a large tarpaulin under her.

She heard her mother's voice from above, "Don't do this to me Mila." At the same time, there was a cracking sound and she was swaying in the air. There were unintelligible shouts and screams followed by more sporadic movements under her. Part of the gutter gave away from its strap and Mila dangled in the wind. The gutter swayed this way then that way before finally breaking away from the roof. Mila fell!

Once again, Mila awoke to the sound of voices, her mother's and a guy called Hayden. Once again, she pretended to be asleep.

Mila listened to their argument. "Oh my God, this is so surreal, I must be dreaming," Mila thought.

Sue Ellen argued that they should leave Mila behind and catch the next flight to Florida. Hayden opposed her by explaining he wants her (Mila) as his daughter because she was perfect for his image. He said, "As soon as she is healed, we will leave for Florida and in the meantime, we will get started on the paperwork to make her our daughter. I will leave it up to you to change her looks!"

Hayden Schneider was a powerful American in his mid-fifties who met Sue Ellen on a cruise in the Caribbean. He immediately liked her go-get-what-you-want attitude. He also admired her ability to mingle with the rich and the famous. He always wanted a child he could groom for his business. Hayden knew his son would always hate him because of the way he treated his son's mother.

After her escape attempt, Mila was heavily guarded. She had no phone because it was taken the same day she was kidnapped. She now had a personal maid. As her ankle healed, a beautician was hired to make Mila look more like a prestigious, young Caucasian woman. Her hair color and style were changed to a short blond bob, but despite the expensive makeover, Mila still held some resemblance to Camila. The paperwork that was the topic of their discussion earlier had finally arrived. Mila now had a new passport which bore her name as Mila Schneider!

A few weeks passed before Mila was taken to Florida. She remembered day at Miami International Airport; she was emotionally weary. She tried to be nice to the young girl who sat next to her on the plane, but she was so distraught, she could not even fake it.

The residence in Florida was even more impressive than the one in Barbados. What caught Mila's attention was how isolated the house was. Trees lined the property as far as the eye could see.

Mila embarked on a plan to starve herself. She thought if she got so sick from starvation, she would be rushed to the hospital. It would be easier for her to slip someone a note about her situation and burst this kidnapping saga wide open.

Mila refused to eat, refused to attend her distance learning and online classes, and refused to communicate with anyone.

On the third day of the starvation plan, Sue Ellen stormed into her room and between clinched teeth told Mila to sit up and listen and listen well because she was not going to repeat herself. Sue Ellen's voice sent shivers down Mila's spine. Mila snapped to attention as she sensed danger.

"I chose you because of your complexion. You are the perfect fit for this family, and you are not going to mess up my plans. You are Mila Schneider and you have to start acting like it! As of today, this business of starving yourself ends."

Mila shouted, "You can't stop me, I am not going to eat your rich food! I want to be back with my real family."

Sue Ellen slowly advanced towards Mila, who now sat up in defiance. Mila clenched a pillow and was ready to throw it.

"Don't test me Mila because I will make you regret this for the rest of your miserable life," said Sue Ellen.
Mila threw the pillow and it smacked Sue Ellen in her face. The sudden impact caused Sue Ellen to take a step back. Sue Ellen snatched the pillow

from the floor and with a sudden leap she had Mila pinned on the bed.

Sue Ellen said, "Do you want your father, the bitch Rachael and your precious sister to be dead tomorrow?"

"Oh God no," Mila screamed to the top of her lungs. "Get off of me; I will do whatever you want!"

Suddenly, footsteps were heard in the hall and the door flew open. Hayden yelled, "Sue Ellen what are you doing?"

Sue Ellen jumped off the bed, brushed passed her husband and slammed the door.

CHAPTER 9

CHAPTER 9

Mila spent hours on her knees praying to God to help her live to see her family again. Finally, she dragged herself under the covers and thought really hard about her situation. She remembered the horrific stories her dad told them about his childhood. She then wondered what her dad would do in her situation. She decided on a plan! She would be the good little daughter for this woman who called herself a mother. Then she would wait for the unguarded moment to make her escape.

The evening was warm, but a lingering breeze blew, encouraging pedestrians to relax their hustle. Hayden took Sue Ellen and Mila out to dinner. Sue Ellen was pleasant but suspicious of Mila's compliant behavior. Hayden was just happy everyone was getting along.

The dinner was quite delicious. There was lemongrass coconut shrimp, Portuguese styled stew fish and Guyanese curried fish. There was polite conversation over dinner. Hayden answered his phone several times for which he apologized and left the table. Mila told herself she would eavesdrop on every conversation, read every note and observe every action. She had to be very careful so she wouldn't get caught.

Sue Ellen watched Mila's every move. She asked for an excuse to go to the bathroom and sure enough, Sue Ellen followed her on a pretext that she would use it also. Mila exited the bathroom before Sue Ellen and as she approached their table, she noticed a young man leaning over Hayden. The expression on Hayden's face was not pleasant. Suddenly the young man turned and stared at Mila, who had stopped in her tracks. He had cold gray, piercing eyes with which he surveyed Mila from head to toe. He then jerked himself from the table and with long strides left the room.

Hayden looked at Mila who quietly sild into her seat. He was just about to explain the presence of the young man when he looked up and saw Sue Ellen. He thought the better of it and said to Mila, "How is your evening going so far?" Mila gave him a trace of a smile and simply said, "Great, thank you!

Mila pretended to focus on her desert but was listening intently to what Hayden said to Sue Ellen, "Erick was here!"

"What?" said Sue Ellen raising her voice, "You told me you would have nothing to do with him. What did he want?"

Mila thought to herself, "I have to pay attention.

Sue Ellen does not like Erick. I wonder who he is? He sure resembles Hayden!"

Hayden stared at Sue Ellen long and hard.

Sue Ellen fidgeted in her chair, twirled her desert dish, took a small sample than said to Mila in a stiff voice, "Your hair looks nice."

Mila held her eyes for a moment then said, "Thanks."

They drove home in silence. A rain cloud was hanging low and just before they turned into the driveway the rain came down with a vengeance. Hayden sheltered Mila with his jacket as they ran for the door. This polite gesture by Hayden caused Sue Ellen to slam the car door with such force that both heads swerved in her direction. She then took careful determined steps towards them, locking Hayden's eyes with her piercing stare.

Sue Ellen entered the house and flung off her wet scarf and kicked off her shoes.

Mila had a sense there was going to be a fight ensuing between Sue Ellen and Hayden, so she headed for her room. She took off her shoes and doubled back, tiptoed into the hallway and hid behind a large planter. She had a great vantage point from where she was hiding.

Hayden Schneider was a tall man with shoulders that spoke of the good old gym days. Looking at him one could assume that in his younger days he was an avid basketball player.

He walked over to Sue Ellen who stood her ground with her hands on her hips and head tilted backwards so she could look him in his face.

"That is my son," Hayden bellowed."

Mila trembled as her hand flew to her mouth to stop a whimper.

"If I want to have a relationship with him, that is my concern; I care about him."

"Well Mila is my daughter and I don't care about her, what I care about is money, lots of money!"

"Sue Ellen, that child is your flesh and blood and you need to treat her as such. I will tell my son what I want to tell him."

"You and I worked together for this. I was the one who planted the idea in your head. You were such a coward Hayden. I knew we could smuggle drugs, store them in the warehouse and then ship them to your clients. Look what we have done for ourselves, he is not going to be a part of this!"

With one quick movement, Hayden grabbed her by the arm and between clenched teeth whispered something in her ear, released his hold and moved towards their room. Sue Ellen sat down, grabbed a pack of cigarettes from her pocketbook and lit up.

Mila quickly moved to her room and took a shower. Later she made notations in her sketchbook in secret code only she could understand.

Morning broke! Mila tidied her room and went in search of her mother. She entered the kitchen and found Hayden drinking coffee. He informed Mila her mother left to go shopping with her friends and she could be gone all day. Mila began to fix herself some breakfast, she asked Hayden if he would like some, but he politely refused. Mila then asked him how she could get her laundry done. Hayden explained the laundry service comes twice a week and she should use the disposal shoot behind her closet to drop her clothes into the laundry room.

Hayden eyed Mila as she bit into her toast. There was sadness in his eyes. He thought, "This is so wrong to take this child from her parents." Hayden was taking a deep look at his life and wondering if it was all worth it. Once, he had loved Sue Ellen so much, but his love began to wane over time when he realized she had become so greedy!

Erick had reached out to Hayden, even though he was still angry about the way Hayden had abandoned him and his mother. So, Hayden made up in his mind he would begin to build a relationship with his son. Hayden left the room to call Erick.

Mila finished her breakfast, tidied the kitchen and set off to check out the laundry shoot. Inserted neatly into the back wall of her closet was a door. She opened it and flicked the switch. About six feet from her closet was a large laundry shoot. Mila thought of exploring it, but she decided to leave it for a later time.

Mila learned, and she learned fast. She knew how clever Sue Ellen could be. Mila never doubted there were cameras strategically placed throughout the house. It seemed as though Hayden had the same thought because when Erick arrived, he met with him in the garden. Mila watched them from her window. Prior to Erick's arrival Hayden told Mila the young man she saw in the restaurant was his son with his first wife.

"I know he hates me, and I don't blame him, I've done some awful things in my time." He suddenly stopped talking and stared through the window. Mila thought maybe he felt as if he had said too much. He then turned back to her and politely asked if she could make him some sandwiches. She did.

Hayden introduced Erick to Mila then stepped away for a minute. They exchanged pleasantries as Mila tried to evade those piercing gray eyes. Hayden returned and Mila escaped to her room.

After weeks of careful investigating, Mila knew where his warehouse was located, the names of four of his drug ring clients and he had almost a million dollars in one bank. She also discovered Sue Ellen might be using cocaine.

The days dragged by slowly, causing Mila to teeter on the brink of depression. She wanted her real family so badly. She was so scared of Sue Ellen after the threat she made on her family.

It was a Sunday evening when the situation in the Schneider's house suddenly took a dramatic turn.

Mila set aside the sketch she was completing of her real family. The feeling of nostalgia was too overbearing. She rolled over and grabbed a novel from her night table. She must have dozed off for something woke her up. There was the slight click again! She turned off her light and slid from between the sheets. She tiptoed to the window. Her eyes swept the front yard, then swept it again. Oh no, there was something there which grabbed her attention. It was something black and shiny. As her pupils adjusted to the dark, she was sure the black shiny thing was a van parked behind a tree next to the electrical pole. Mila eyes climbed the pole and she held her breath. Someone was moving on the pole! At the same time, she was wrangling with her thoughts there was a loud crash of the front door. She sprung from the window and headed for her bedroom door. She stopped in her tracks.

The events of that night will live with Mila forever. Hayden was the first one to be gunned-down as he dashed out to investigate the crashing sound. The impact of the bullets caused him to levitate; he hung in the air then crashed to the floor. He was dead. Sue Ellen's screams were cut short when her face was blown off. Mila did not wait to see more. Her feet took wings as she flew across her room. Her mind raced like clockwork. She grabbed two sheets from off the bed and knotted them together. She opened a window and threw one end outside while anchoring the other end on the windowsill. She then grabbed her sneakers and her pair of jeans from out the hamper and ran to her closet. She could hear them coming up the steps to her room. Her heart rammed against her chest, causing her breath to explode in torrents.

Quickly she changed in the little space, then without hesitation, she dropped her body down the laundry shoot. She landed in the huge laundry basket bulging with dirty linens. Her hands were shaking, and her legs were wobbly.

"Where do I go next," she thought. She could hear them wrecking her room.

"Find the girl," said a familiar voice she could not place.

The room was dark, and she felt her way to the door. She found the door and slowly opened it. The door squeaked and she stood still. After holding her breath for a while, she eased her body into the hallway. She took a few steps when suddenly her head exploded then everything went black.

CHAPTER 10

CHAPTER 10

Camila and Sofia searched the internet to find more information about the Schneider's murders. They were eager to see if they could find out something about Mila. Finally, they learned a   part-time housekeeper said there was a young girl living in the house and her name was Mila.

Camila left to use the bathroom. Sofia was in a low mood, thinking of her son and his children and wondering if their lives would ever be normal again. Tears stung her eyes as she bemoaned her painful history. Suddenly there was a knock on the kitchen door. Sofia sprang up. Jane arrived in her usual happy mood. She sailed into the kitchen after greeting Sofia and asked for Camila. Before Sofia could respond, Jane sat in Camila's seat in front of the computer.

"Oh My God, Isn't this horrible? I can't believe what is happening! One of my friends told me his parents know this family and there is a son and maybe a daughter. My friend said the son is Hayden's and the daughter is his wife's."

Camila had quietly returned from the bathroom and heard the end of Jane's statement. Camila could not keep it together any longer. She collapsed in tears onto the floor.

Sofia and Jane were able to calm Camila down by administering a mild sedative and tucked her into Sofia's large comfortable sofa.

* * * *

After Sofia moved into the neighborhood, she became friendly with the neighbors next door. They were from Puerto Rico. They were Jane's parents. About two years ago, they decided to move back to their home country to start a business there. Jane finally decided to live in the house after she became a teacher. She had been Sofia's little best friend ever since. Sofia could not help herself, she told Jane about Mila. She trusted Jane. She then went on to explain what they think might have happened to Mila. Jane was in shock! She felt as if she were watching a lifetime movie.

When Camila woke up, they decided on an action plan. First, they would have to be very careful. Second, they would hold off giving the latest details to Sam or Rachael. Third, they would pretend Camila was a foreign student journalist to see what other information they could find. Jane made her credentials looked legitimate and supplied her with probing questions that would glean the right answers. Camila would never be left alone

Jane promised she would always be around.

There was a press conference scheduled at Hayden's office the next day, so the girls prepared by role-playing. Sofia begged them to be careful because she would not be able to face her son if something happened to Camila.

Camila looked the part of a student journalist. She wore a beautiful navy suit Jane loaned her, moderate heels for comfort, a tape recorder and her notebook. Sofia and Jane were impressed.

She took her seat in the area provided for all journalists. The conference began. Many questions were asked about Hayden's business. What products he held in his warehouse? Where did the products come from? Was there anything illegal involved? Was there a business partner or partners?

Camila cleared her throat, stood up and asked, "Can you tell us about the young girl who lived in the house with Mr. and Mrs. Schneider?"

The business manager was caught off guard for a moment. He made a small cough, composed himself, looked at Camila and said, "Yes, there was a girl who was part of the family." Suddenly there were a lot of voices, all trying to find out more about this new revelation.

The manager eyed the crowed, swallowed then said, "The only information we can give at this time about the young lady is that she is the daughter of Mrs. Schneider."

Jane watched Camila from the far corner of the room and saw her body go limp and her face ashen. Jane was about to move towards her when Camila slowly pulled herself up and applied her breathing technique. She was ready with the next probing question.

"Can you tell me sir, where that young lady is now?" Camila's heart was racing, as she prayed for her sister to be alive. The manager said he was passing the mike over to the officer handling the case.

The officer introduced himself as Detective Fernandez as he exchanged places with the manager. He seriously looked around the room at the group of people, his eyes found Camila's.

"This is an ongoing investigation and we cannot divulge any specifics at this time, but we can safely say only two bodies were found at the residence of the Schneider's.

Camila's slender frame was shaking when Jane

got to her. She wrapped her arms around her and walked her to the car. "No news is good news," said Jane. "We will find your sister! Tomorrow we will visit the library and see what we can dig up."

Camila said, "Thanks Jane, you are a wonderful friend."

CHAPTER 11

CHAPTER 11

Sofia was doing her own investigation at the hospital where she worked. Many staff members knew of the businessman and two doctors had some ugly stories to tell. They reminded Sofia about the six teenagers who were brought into the hospital with opioid overdose. Residents in the area claimed the serious mix of bad drugs came from Hayden's warehouse. Two of the children died, one was in coma for months. Eventually he had to be taken off the respirator. Two of the students have different degrees of brain damage. It was only one who walked away unscathed.

One of the doctors reminded them of the Polony twins. He said, "Remember how hard we worked that night to save those young men, but we failed. Word is - all these incidents originated from the drugs that were shipped through the Schneider's warehouse."

"I cannot believe this, it is horrible," Sofia said.

"But wait a minute" said one nurse, "Remember the kid who ate some of his father's stash and got violently sick?"

"Yes, the little black kid from the Southside!"

Answered another.

"That's the one! Now that child was really lucky, lucky his mother found him just in the nick of time," said one of the nurses.

As Sofia worked through her shift, she had a lot of information to mull over. Sofia wondered how her innocent granddaughter could be caught up in a situation like this. "Well," Sofia thought, "rephrase; not caught up but thrust into a situation like this? It is that Sue Ellen. "Sammy I am so sorry you met that devil woman," she thought.

That night on her way home Sofia begged God to watch over her little "nieta," she tried not to cry as she got behind the wheel. "I have to be stronger," she told herself.

Sofia got home and started dinner when the girls came in. They helped Sofia and the three sat down as Sofia brought out a bottle of her famous Stella Rosa Moscato wine.

Jane described to Sofia how well Camila handled herself at the Schneider's warehouse press conference, but the big question remained, "Where is Mila?"

Camila said, "Let's look at facts, only two bodies

were found, Hayden's and Sofia's, fact! The manager stated there was a young girl who lived in the house, fact! That girl was the daughter of Sue Ellen Schneider, fact. The part-time housekeeper said the young girl's name was Mila, fact!"

Jane interrupted with a question, "Do you think Mila might have escaped?"

"That's a credible assumption," Camila said then paused for a second. "I wonder if there are any hiding places around the residence like an old hut, barrels or anything to hide in?"

Jane added, "It would not hurt to drive around the residence, what you think Sofia?" Sofia was at work since five that morning and after the wine she was half asleep.

Camila noticed how her grandmother's eyes were closing and encouraged her to take a nap. Just then the phone rang. It was Rachael!

Sofia answered and exchanged pleasantries. She explained to Rachael how rough her shift was because two nurses called out. Rachael encouraged her to go take a nap. As Sofia handed the phone to Camila, she whispered, "Don't say anything about Mila." Camila gave Sofia thumbs, up and signaled for her to go to bed.

After ending the phone call, the two girls checked on Sofia, she was sound asleep. They secured the house and headed for the Schneider's residence.

They were surprised at the vastness of the lot! It took them a while to drive around the building. It was an awesome house. As they drove around the second time, they looked for any structure or container Mila might have used as a safe haven. There was nothing on the property that could have given Mila such comfort.

There was police tape that cordoned off a section of the front area. As the girls slowly crawled around for the third time, they noticed a footpath to the side of the building. They carefully parked the car behind an overgrown hedge. They surveyed the area carefully before exiting the car. They stayed together as they stepped cautiously along the footpath. The footpath led them to the front of the building. They rounded the corner of the house, which was secluded from the street by thick evergreen trees. Suddenly they heard a sound. They held their breaths and shrunk low behind the bushes. There was the sound again.

"Oh my God," said Camila, "we cannot get caught!"

As footsteps came up the driveway, the girls retreated further into the hedge. Suddenly someone stepped into the clearing, it was the mailman. The girls remained hidden until he left. They resumed their sleuthing. They walked slowly keeping themselves obscured, while looking for any clues that would lead them to Mila.

"There is nothing here," uttered Jane, just then Camila said. "Look, look Jane."
Jane spun around thinking it might be a snake. She was scared of snakes. "Do you see it?" asked Camila.

Almost hidden behind a clump of grass was one sneaker laying with its bottom up. Jane reached for it. She picked it up and turned to give it to Camila. Camila's face was ashen. She took two shaky steps, bent over and threw up her lunch behind a rosebush.

CHAPTER 12

CHAPTER 12

Hayden grew up in money! His dad was a banker and his mom was a nurse. He was the type of guy who always lived large; lots of friends, parties and sports. During his college days, he was a great basketball player. He was a popular guy, always spending money, and always footing the bills for drinks and food.

During his later college years, he met Julie. She was studying agriculture science. Julie came from a family of farmers in South Carolina and hoped to pursue her dreams as a modern-day farmer. Their relationship grew over time but not serious enough for him to follow her back to South Carolina. After college, Julie returned home and made a big change to farming in her hometown of Manning. She became a professor at a nearby college. She devoted lots of time with individuals who worked the land. She taught them how to use modern technology to produce bountiful crops.

Hayden was drafted to play in the NBA for a team in North Carolina. He was a rising star when his career came to a sudden halt. He suffered a severe injury to his right leg which rendered him unfit to continue his lifelong dream of playing professional basketball.

Julie visited Hayden at his parents' home in Virginia while he healed from his injury. Hayden and his parents really enjoyed Julie's company. His dad was fascinated by the stories Julie told of how technology made agriculture more manageable with high profit yields. Mrs. Schneider thought Julie was a lovely, intelligent lady.

Their distance relationship continued over several months when finally, the decided to tie the knot. Within two years, Julie gave birth to a boy they named Erick.

CHAPTER 13

CHAPTER 13

Situations began to change quickly in the lives of these newlyweds.

Developers moved into Julie's hometown and started to buy up acres and acres of farmland. Their intent was to create a holiday resort. Their argument was about the location being ideal because of the beautiful lake, lush vegetation, and the accessibility of I-95 that threads through many states.

As time passed, Julie lost her desire to becoming a great innovator. Hayden became the coach at the local high school but in his heart, he knew this job was not for him. They secured a comfortable cottage on the outskirts of town.

For Hayden, something seemed to be missing. He often longed for old times. The happy times he spent at parties with friends and drinks. The thoughts were always alive in his head.

One cold November evening Hayden's mother passed away. Hayden felt as if his life was unravelling. To compound his grief, he had to move his father into a nursing home. This young family had to make some difficult decisions. Hayden wanted to be near his dad because there was no one else in Virginia to take care of him. However, Julie felt grounded in South Carolina and was finding it very difficult to entertain the thought of moving.

Julie finally made the move to Virginia. She obtained a job at a high school as an agricultural/science teacher. Hayden became a coach at a nearby YMCA. They decided to rent out the house in South Carolina and remodeled his parents' house in which they lived.

Hayden was running late for work one morning when he got the phone call from the nursing home. His father had passed.

Hayden's life began to take a different turn after the passing of his father. He started drinking and staying out late, hanging at bars and rough houses with friends. He ignored Julie's complaints about his behavior.

Then the inevitable happened! Julie awoke one morning, and Hayden was gone.

At first, Julie thought perhaps something serious had happened to Hayden. She called everyone she knew who might have information of his whereabouts. The responses were all negative until she called his real estate lawyer.

The information Julie got from the lawyer filled her heart with so much pain, she was ill for a long time. Hayden was not coming back! He had asked the lawyer to oversee all transactions for the sale of his house as soon as Julie moved out.

Julie's illness overshadowed what was happening to little Erick. He was devastated! His little heart had turned to stone. He vowed never to forgive his father for what he did to him and his mom. He secretly promised himself he would take his father out when he became grown.

CHAPTER 14

CHAPTER 14

Julie moved back to Manning, South Carolina and began to pick up the pieces of her life. With her background in agriculture she landed a job as a research development specialist with the company, turning farmland into holiday resorts.

Julie decided she had to be resilient and move on with her life. She was thankful she did not sell her house. She and Erick moved back home.

Erick, who was now ten years old and did not fare well after losing his father, had a rough time settling down in school. After being labeled as oppositional and defiant, he was placed in a special needs class. At first the services rendered stabilized Erick, but as time went by Julie was always in a constant battle trying to control Erick's behavior. Then one day things changed.

Erick was home alone when the phone call came. It was Hayden! When Erick heard his voice, he dropped the phone as if it had bit him. He stared at it for a long time then gingerly reached down and picked it up.

"What do you want?" asked Erick

"I am sorry son, for what I did many years ago!"

Just listening to his father's voice slowly brought Erick's blood to a boil and he started to hyperventilate. He knew he was going to lose control and lose control he did. He ripped the phone from the wall after barking into the receiver, "You are a dead man!"

Young Erick laid on the sofa, sneakers and all, just staring at the ceiling. He laid there for a long time. This kid was weighed down with the heavy thoughts of a man. After a long time of thinking, he stared his future in the face, realizing the only way to destroy his father was to change his behavior.

True to his promise, Erick worked hard at home and school. He made better grades and he played basketball, baseball and soccer. Julie was so proud of her son. That day she came home, she knew something had changed in Erick. She supported Erick in every way she could. She also made sure he attended his weekly counseling sessions.

CHAPTER 15

CHAPTER 15

Hayden sold his parents' house and travelled abroad. On one of his trips he met a beautiful woman named Sue Ellen, she was from Barbados.

On his first visit to Barbados Hayden fell in love with the island. He brought a warehouse and went into the warehousing business. With the support of Sue Ellen his business started to make huge profits. He bought an old plantation house on a large lot on the eastern side of the island. Hayden refurbished the house. After divorcing Julie, he married Sue Ellen and began a new life in Barbados.

Despite all his achievements Hayden felt guilty about over the way he treated Julie and Erick. He could still hear the anguish in Erick's threat when he made that phone call. He hoped someday he would be able to make it up to Julie and Erick.

Little did Hayden know; Julie had moved on with her life! She had met Roland but initially did not encourage his persistent advances because she was so preoccupied with Erick. However, since Erick was holding fast to his promises of doing better, she began to accept Roland's affection.

* * * *

Years passed! Hayden was encouraged by the success of his business, so he bought another warehouse, but this time in Florida. Sue Ellen had taken a serious interest in the warehousing business. Many times he wondered why she was so involved until it was revealed to him she was running cocaine through the Florida warehouse.

Hayden was shocked! Sue Ellen's racketeering in his business had thrown him for a loop. He loved this woman and enjoyed her company more than ever, but her behavior was giving him pause. During her confession, he admitted he was surprised at the rate at which his monetary success exploded.

Hayden and Sue Ellen had a long discussion about the drugs in the warehouse. Sue Ellen was able to convince him if they remained careful and picked the right people to support them, they could do even better with the warehouse in Florida.

CHAPTER 16

CHAPTER 16

Sofia decided she should inform Sam about the unfolding situation in Florida.

Sam was beside himself with worry. After he hung up the phone, he contacted the airline to book his flight, but his frustration was compounded by another setback. He found out his passport was expired and the process to have it updated would take four weeks to be completed.

Sam immediately reached out to all his friends who had contacts to the passport office for help in reducing the processing time for his passport renewal. Finally, he got the processing time reduced to three weeks.

In the meantime, whenever they spoke on the phone, Rachael used all her comforting skills to divert Camila's mind from the looming crisis.

"Mama Rachael do you remember when you bought Mila and me those white sneakers with pink laces?" Camila asked.

"Yes baby, I do remember!" Rachel answered.

"Ma, Mila and I loved those sneakers so much. I was wearing my pair when I left Barbados, and apparently Mila was wearing hers when she was taken," Camila said.

Sam met with Detective Rodrick and updated him on the latest developments concerning Mila. The next day Detective Rodrick contacted the Miami police precinct in the area of the Schneider's residence about the missing girl's case. The Miami detective promised he would call back with developments on the case.

Detective Fernandez was the Miami detective. He was in his early to late fifties; a pleasant man with sandy gray hair and a positive demeanor. He kept his word. He called back later with a tiny lead explaining a pizza parlor attendant who was on his way home from work, heard a girl's screams as he drove pass the Schneider's home around the same time of the murders.

The detective promised he would continue to work this case. He needed Camila and Jane to see him first the next day. He asked them to bring the sneaker and any other piece of clothing of Mila's.

* * * *

The next day, Detective Fernandez was reassuring after Camila broke down while explaining the details of Mila's disappearance. He promised he would delve deeper into the double homicide and he would give them daily updates. Camila turned over the sneaker and a tee shirt which belonged to Mila. The detective said the forensics department needed to have Mila's DNA on file.

The Schneider's residence was again searched by the forensic crew with a focus on the room, presumably Mila's. There was a DNA match that proved Mila Duncan/Schneider was an occupant of that house.

Camila and Sofia were again called back to the station to identify some of Mila's belongings. Upon arriving at the station, Camila and Sofia were ushered into a room of glass with unusual apparatuses everywhere. The room made them nervous. They were afraid of what they might uncover.

The forensic specialist had them look at many pieces of Mila's clothing, shoes, jewelry and her sketchbook. At the top of the book Mila wrote, "My real family." The drawing clearly showed Sam, Rachael Camila and Mila.

"How old is your sister?" asked the specialist.
"Sixteen," replied Camila.

Looking through the sketchbook, the specialist commented, "This is great work.

"Yea, I know, she has murals hanging in our school back in Barbados," Camila replied.

Sofia said, "My granddaughter was born with an amazing talent."

"Yes, I see," replied the specialist

Camila and Sofia could not identify anything else of Mila's except for the work in her sketchbook. With heavy hearts they left the room and were headed to the main lobby when suddenly they heard someone quickly approaching. They turned only to see the specialist with Mila's sketchbook.

"Hey ladies hold up for a minute," said the specialist. Sofia and Camila stopped and waited.

"Camila, could you take Mila's sketchbook home and peruse it for any clues? You never know, even the smallest detail may help us," said the specialist.

They thanked the expert and left.

CHAPTER 17

CHAPTER 17

Jane saw the demeanor of her friends and decided to take them out to dinner. She took them to a Spanish restaurant, La Comida, Jane's favorite place to eat and unwind. The restaurant was owned by friends of her parents. It was a warm and welcoming place.

Sofia, Camila, and Jane discussed the events of the day and tried to create scenarios that would shed light on Mila's whereabouts.

"I wonder if she was picked up by anyone?" asked Jane.

"That's a thought because the detective said connected to her bedroom was an old antique laundry shoot and it appeared as if Mila used it to get away." Sofia explained.

Camila then suggested they make flyers and post them around the neighborhood.

"Great idea," said Jane. "Hey we can start with this restaurant!"

The next day while Sofia was at work the girls printed flyers of Mila and posted them around the neighborhood where the Schneiders lived.

Just as they entered Sofia's cottage the phone rang. Camila answered. The female on the other end was speaking Spanish with a heavy accent. She was very excited. Camila handed the phone to Jane.

Jane's entire demeanor changed. She suddenly sprang into action as she, said "gracias, gracias, Maria," and hung up.

Jane said softly, "Follow me!"

The two girls were out of the house, back in the car speeding towards the Spanish restaurant. As they travelled, Jane told her that one of the employees at the La Comida has a cousin who worked on the Schneider's place about two weeks ago and he remembers the girl on the flyer.

The girls were quickly and secretly escorted into a small back room. On a wooden bench with his back against the wall and hands crossed over his chest sat a nervous Spanish gentleman.

Jane smiled warmly as she greeted him in Spanish. He did the same, adding he also spoke English. He said his name was Hector. The girls moved their chairs closer to him and Jane introduced Camila and herself.

Hector explained that his boss asked him to complete a job at the Schneider's residence. He continued to tell how his boss took sick that day and he needed someone he could trust to take his place. There were other workers there performing other tasks, but his job was to cut the bushes and remove trash. He was trimming the hedges and hauling the debris to his truck when he looked up and saw a young girl climbing out of a window. The same girl on the flyer!

"My heart stopped," Hector explained, as he placed his hand over his chest. "I was scared, I yelled and as I did, the girl fell and rolled down the slanted roof. She was screaming and everyone started running to help her, then she grabbed onto the gutter that gave away and she was swaying in the air." At that point Hector stood up and swayed his body to interject emphasis.

Camila's hands were clasped over her mouth and her eyes were huge ovals in her head. Jane moved over to Camila and hugged her tightly.

Hector continued, "The other workers grabbed ladders to get to her, but she was too high up. I got the large tarpaulin and we held it under her. She was saved.

Camila was crying softly! Jane reached into her

purse and gave the man a twenty-dollar bill. His eyes lit up as he kept saying "gracias, gracias!"

"De nada, de nada," Jane uttered who assumed the meeting was over, but Hector leaned forward and whispered that he heard of bad drugs that were in the warehouse. He wished someone could do something about it because many people are getting sick from it.

The girls thanked Hector and begged him to stay in touch.

They drove in silence!

Back at Sofia's house, Camila wrapped her arms around herself and anchored herself to the kitchen wall. She was in a daze. She was wondering to herself if this is how an out of body experience feels like. She listened as Jane called Detective Fernandez and recounted the exact details of the meeting with Hector.

CHAPTER 18

CHAPTER 18

Mila hobbled across the room. She firmly tested the walls, prodding for holes and cracks. It was a frustrating task because she only had on one sneaker and the lump on her head felt like a football. She tried not to think of the pain as she poked a weak spot in the wall with her index finger. Some of the sediment came loose. She tried again, nothing happened. She slowly searched the room for anything that could help puncture a hole in the structure. The light in the room was so dim that what was not visible had to be recognized by the sense of touch. She found nothing. Tears stung her eyes, but she brushed them away. She paused as she thought of her father and what he endured as a child. Her dad was a survivor and she will be too.

She quickly limped over to the cot and ripped the covering off. She was hoping to find a piece of skinny metal that could work as a tool. With the aid of the dim light she traced out the frame of the cot. Her fingers touched something loose. One of the bolts had come loose from a metal strap that anchored the head of the bed to its sides.

Mila worked on it for a while, tugging it back and forth until the strap came loose. Just as Mila moved towards the wall, she heard footsteps. She sprang into action, grabbing the old sheet from the floor and positioned herself on the cot.

The door swung open and a middle-aged woman placed a bowl on the bed. She turned her head to Mila and said, "Eat!" The woman left, locking the door.

Mila did not know that she was so hungry until she smelled the coffee. She ate the two stale biscuits and drank the black coffee. She then continued her work on the wall. Eventually she dislodged enough for her to peek through.

What she saw caused her to rip off her shirt and stuff it in her mouth to prevent herself from screaming. She was locked in a hut not far from a docking area. She saw two big boats and girls! Many girls dressed in rags being prodded along the docks. Mila knew right away she was caught up in a human trafficking ring.

She carefully examined the door to her prison. She thanked God for the days she spent helping her father build the garage and work on his taxis. She realized the hinges of the door were screwed into a wooden facing and that facing was worn out by termite invasion. Mila stripped the cot again and found a sturdier piece of metal that was just right to dislodge the door.

She worked on the door for hours, she wanted to get it off before night fall, and she did. She decided that under the cover of darkness, she would make her move.

CHAPTER 19

CHAPTER 19

Sofia had just stepped out of the shower when the phone rang. It was Detective Fernandez.

"Hello Ms. Sofia," said Detective Fernandez.

"Hello detective," said Sofia.

"I am sorry, but I have to hand over Mila's case to another detective because of some personal problems. I will be out of Miami for couple of weeks."

"Oh no detective, the girls have some new leads and would like to share them with you," said Sofia.

Detective Fernandez said, "Don't worry Ms. Sofia there is a very smart young detective who will be taking over all of my cases until I return. You will be in capable hands. His name is Edward Saunders. I will let him know you will be stopping by tomorrow to update him on the new leads. By the way, do you still have my card?"

"I do," replied Sofia.

"On the back of that card I wrote my cell number, call me if you need to," he said.

"Thank you detective," Sofia said.

* * * *

The next day, Sofia and Jane stopped by to introduce themselves to the new detective. Camila had a headache, so Sofia gave her a Tylenol and told her to rest.

Detective Saunders was very mild mannered. He was tall and handsome, in a scrappy kind of a way. He had piercing gray eyes that held a steady stare. Jane and Sofia explained how they posted flyers of Mila which resulted in the phone call then the meeting with Hector. Jane told every detail of the story she remembered. The detective expressed grave concern. Then Jane, in a hushed voice, told about the drugs stored in the Schneider's warehouse. He took rapid notes as she spoke. Jane finally ended her story. They all took a deep breath at the same time.

Detective Saunders said, "I will get the officers on this right now, thank you ladies!"

Throughout the meeting in Detective Saunders' office, Sofia detected a subtle spark in the detective's eyes as his gaze lingered on Jane.

Sofia told Jane of her intuition regarding Detective Sanders. Jane blushed and laughed it off.

Camila was up when they returned home and was feeling much better.

* * * *

The next day was Sofia's day off. She decided to treat Camila to some new clothes. Grandma and granddaughter had a great time together. They were able to compare and contrast their similarities and differences in colors, types of foods and hobbies. They had a great time together.

CHAPTER 20

CHAPTER 20

Night fell and Mila made her move. She flattened her body through the space she had created and stood still. She listened as her eyes slowly swept the area for any movement. Dim lights that hung on the boats swayed from side to side, keeping the rhythm of the waves. Soft voices filled with pain lingered in the night's air. It was ominous!

Suddenly, Mila dropped to the ground, fading behind a large rock. A girl, who might be in her early teens with a Spanish accent appeared on the deck of one of the boats, she was screaming and begging for help as she tried to leap off the boat. She was apprehended by supposedly a body guard who took her back into the boat.

Mila was galvanized into action by what she just saw. She ripped off pieces of the sheet and wrapped them around her naked foot. She then wrapped extra pieces around her arms and legs. She secured the door shut, thinking, "this will buy me some time." Mila then walked quickly towards the lush terrain where she and the trees became one.

Mila had walked almost half a mile into the woods. A weak moon poked fingers of jagged light through the trees, giving her just enough light to carefully move through the understory.

Mila strategically dropped pieces of the sheet as she moved along. Her plan was to give the appearance of escaping through the woods, but her main intention was to return to the boatyard and help free some of the girls. Mila returned to the boatyard.

* * * *

Back in Florida, Camila lay quietly, studying Mila's drawing. She checked details from different angles when she figured out there were messages skillfully embedded as in a hidden picture. There were four detailed messages. One, Hayden's son Erick hated him. Two, this son is in law enforcement. Three, Sue Ellen abused cocaine and four, Hayden had fights with Sue Ellen over his son.

Camila made documentations of her findings and she also saved the information on her phone and computer.

Sofia arrived from work earlier than expected. Camila was thrilled her grandma was home so they could call the detective about the new discoveries.

Sofia called Detective Edward Saunders.

Detective Saunders promised to send an officer to Sofia's house the next day to collect the information and to follow up on any other leads. Sofia and Camila were grateful for his prompt and sincere response.

CHAPTER 21

CHAPTER 21

Sofia left for work the next day making sure Camila had all the information for the officer. Sofia later texted Camila around lunch time but Camila did not respond. Sofia just knew Camila was busy on her computer or taking a nap.

Hours later, Sofia arrived home, parked her car, entered the house through the garage and called for Camila. She got no answer, so she called again as she walked through the kitchen. Sofia stopped, riveted to the floor. Her hand flew to her chest. She could feel her heart drumming in the soles of her feet.

"Oh God," she screamed as she felt herself falling. She yelled, "Someone took my nieta, help!"

Kitchen chairs were knocked around, a broken teacup was on the floor. Sofia tried to compose herself. She grabbed her pocketbook and found her phone. She called Camila, she waited then she almost flew out of her skin because on the floor next to the trash bin was a dishcloth. The dishcloth lit up when Camila's phone started ringing.

Sofia knew not to touch anything because she didn't want to disturb any potential clues. She called Jane, who was just leaving the nail salon. She told Sofia to stay put and she would be there in a few minutes.

CHAPTER 22

CHAPTER 22

Mila made her way back to the docks. She was tired and hungry. She had scratches on her face and arms which resulted from her ploughing through the undergrowth. The lights from the big boats allowed her to search for the perfect hiding place. She thought about hiding in the bushes, but she decided against that. Even the idea of hiding behind one of the ruined buildings did not give her comfort. Mila wanted to find a hiding place where she could see the area where the girls were being held and to keep an eye on the boats.

Mila found her hiding place! Approximately twenty yards away from the first boat there were some large wooden pillars sticking out of the water at varying heights. Poking through the top of the pillars were rusty giant nails and bent rebars. Mila lowered herself into the water and swam to the pillars. Good luck for her, two of the pillars formed a shelf and above the shelf were two large warped planks that gave her enough space for the perfect cover. Mila hauled herself up, thinking she would be able to keep vigil on the prison guards while waiting for the right moment to free the girls. During her confinement, Mila had lost sense of date and time. She tried to keep track by the daylight and night.

CHAPTER 23

CHAPTER 23

It was early morning. Camila was dragged from the van and tossed to the ground. Detective Saunders barked at one of his subordinates, "take her and lock her up!" Just as she was being hauled to her feet, a middle-aged woman ran out from a nearby shed. She was flapped her hands and screamed, "she is gone, she is gone!"

The detective advanced to the running woman who stopped when she saw her boss. She dropped to her knees, begging him to understand it was not her fault the girl had escaped. What happened next, Camila and Mila will always remember for the rest of their lives.

Detective Saunders pulled his gun from the back of his waistband and shot the woman in her head. She died before she fell.

Mila must have fallen asleep because she awoke to a loud noise. Then there was silence. Mila moved her head towards the direction of the blasting sound and was horrified at what she saw. The girl shaking in fear was her sister Camila, the man who fired the shot was Erick and the dead woman was the woman who brought her breakfast yesterday.

Mila's body convulsed in fear! She was really scared for Camila. She grabbed onto a protruding rebar to keep herself from falling into the water. She prayed, then prayed some more!

Erick, aka Detective Saunders, aka boss yelled, "Let this be a lesson, anyone disobeys me this will be your end." He pointed to the woman's body. "Get rid of her, throw her in the river and lock this one up. The runaway will never make it."

Mila kept her eyes on Camila. She needed to be able to identify the hut where they were taking Camila because tonight, she would rescue her sister.

Erick walked over to the first boat and told the captain within two days; they would be shipping out.

"Ok boss," said the captain with a mixture of fear and anger.

Erick checked on the other prisoners, fired some bullets in the air then left. There was an eerie quietness that dropped over the boatyard. It was like everyone was wrangling with his or her thoughts of what just transpired. The captain came on deck with three cell phones.

He dialed and began to recount what just took

place. "The boss man es muy loco!" he said, "after this run, I will call it quits! I can't believe he killed Isabella!"

Suddenly there was a flurry of movements. Two girls got up on deck and plunged off the boat. The captain dropped his phones and rushed to the other end of the vessel.

"It's now or never," Mila whispered.

Mila lowered herself into the water and without a sound climbed up the rope ladder, grabbed a phone and was back in the water moving against the waves with the phone held above the surface.

CHAPTER 24

CHAPTER 24

Jane arrived and rushed over to Sofia! Sofia was in bad shape. Her tears flowed as she held her head and rocked from side to side. Her cries reflected a pain buried so deep and now was cruelly uncovered. Jane hugged her best friend and fought really hard to hold back her own tears.

Jane said, "Listen, I was thinking, since the new detective took over the case, we've not received and information or updates. Maybe he is too inexperienced, or he lacks the passion for solving the case like Detective Fernandez had. So let's call Detective Fernandez, remember he gave you his cell number."

Sofia wiped her eyes and began to compose herself. Jane handed her a glass of water when Camila's phone rang. Jane froze! Sofia dropped the glass of water. Jane got to the phone.

"Camila, Camila!" Jane screamed.

"Grandma Sofia," Mila said, Jane handed the phone to Sofia.

"Oh mi nieta," then Sofia stopped talking as her eyes slowly enlarged in her head. "Mila, Oh my God, gracias Dios!"

Mila took a chance and dialed her sister's phone, but she was ready to ditch the stolen phone if she heard Erick's voice because she knew he would be able to track her. Her move paid off! She was able to brief Sofia about their precarious situation and what her plans were. Mila took some pictures of the boatyard and texted them to her grandma.

"Grandma, I intend to free Camila and we will be making our way west towards the bushes. Grandma, there are so many girls held here on two boats and in little nasty huts. I will leave this phone where the cops can track it to this horrible place."

Suddenly, Mila's voice was hushed. She whispered as she cupped the phone to her mouth, "we love you grandma, pray for us."

The captain was back on the boat after removing the girls from the water. He picked up the two other phones and started to look for the third one. Finally, he gave up with a jester which signaled he might have dropped it in the water.

CHAPTER 25

CHAPTER 25

During her months of captivity Mila was always on high alert. She learned to pay attention to everything around her because she knew even the inconsequential detail could save her life. She knew where the shadows fell when night closed in. She knew to get to this place, one had to travel on a dirt road; the mud on Erick's tires told her so. She also knew Erick would not hesitate to murder her and her sister. So as she slid from her perch the paramount thoughts were to move quietly, swiftly and safely.

Mila was at Camila's hut within seconds. She hunkered in a dark triangle as she observed the lock on Camila's hut. She listened with bated breath as she analyzed the best approach. Mila realized fortunately for them; Camila's door was not locked. The padlock was just laced through the hasp. With precision she slipped the padlock out of the hasp and slowly eased the door open. Mila tensed as a weak ray of light came through the crack. Mila blocked it with her body. Within seconds Mila was in the room with the door shut. Camila sprang upright with a gasp. With lightning speed Mila had her hand over her sister's mouth and whispered in her ear. Camila threw her arms around her sister and buried her face in the angle of her neck and quietly sobbed. "We have to get moving," Mila whispered.

The girls arranged the bed covers to look like a sleeping person. Mila replaced the padlock just the way it was. They took the lamp and set it in an old bucket and covered the bucket with Camila's shirt. They circled the perimeter of the darkness and made it to the undergrowth.

The girls were so frightened that they moved quickly through the bushes without speaking. Mila led the way, holding the lamp as a torch to light their path. Their focus was so much on escaping, they were oblivious to the dangers surrounding them. At one point they jumped right over a large snake. Camila walked right into a large spider web, which made her cry out so loudly, they were thrown into a nervous panic, thinking they might be caught. They covered the lamp with leaves and hid behind some old discarded wine barrels. They used large sheets of tree bark to fend off the annoying mosquitoes. The eerie sounds of the woods by night would stay with the girls for a long time.

Finally, they stopped behind a huge banyan tree. Camila rubbed her right shoulder as she explained how she found the recorded messages in Mila's drawing.

"Mila you are so clever, I found the messages

and Grandma Sofia and I called Detective Saunders to report our findings. He promised he would send someone over to collect the drawings. I was surprised when he showed up at the back door. I let him in and showed him what I found. Suddenly he grabbed me and was trying to put a towel over my face. I knocked the towel out of his hand and tried to make it to the front door. As I slipped behind the kitchen island, I dropped my phone and tossed a dishcloth over it. I did not want him to get my phone because I saved all the information on my phone as backup," said Camila.

Mila held her sister's face with her hands and wiped away her tears. Camila sobbed and choked as she continued to tell of her kidnapping.

"Mila, he caught me by my hair and dragged me back to the kitchen, and then there was blackness. I awoke when I was dumped from his car in that horrible boatyard," Camila sobbed.

The girls continued to move through the woods. By Camila's watch the girls had walked for about two hours and were overcome by fatigue. Camila found a long flat rock which they used as a cutting tool to clear their path for easier access to the unknown. They decided to trek on.

CHAPTER 26

CHAPTER 26

Julie sensed a change in her son Erick's behavior since she told him she opened his mail by mistake and discovered he had applied for a name change. She knew he was changing jobs and was moving out of state, but she didn't know what to make of his distant behavior.

Julie was really proud of her son! He graduated from high school and went on to college. She and Roland, her new husband, were really impressed by the way he turned out. Roland owned a used car lot and during school breaks Erick helped out around the lot. The two guys really enjoyed each other's company. They talked about many things from fishing to boating to girls. However, one thing Erick never liked to talk about was his father.

Julie expressed her concerns to her husband late one night as they watched T.V. and ate ice cream. "Ro, I think something is going on with Erick. Would you believe he changed his entire name to Edward Saunders? I mean, you'd think if a person was going to change their name it would be the last name, not his whole name, right?" she asked.

"You are right, I noticed a change too. He is more pensive and shorter tempered. Jules you know I try to be supportive in any way I can, so I was trying to encourage him to patch things up with his real dad and before you know it, he threw a Snapple bottle across the office breaking a window," Roland said.

CHAPTER 27

CHAPTER 27

Sofia was obligated to let her son know what was happening with his two daughters. She dreaded the phone call she had to make but she made it anyway. Sam exerted every effort to stay positive on the phone with his mother because he knew if he broke down, she may not recuperate from this horrible experience unfolding in their lives. Before he hung up, he assured her everything would be alright.

Sam ran to his room grabbed his shirt and dressed as he made it to his car. He got to the police station in 10 minutes flat. Fortunately, Sergeant Rodrick was in his office. The sergeant was on the phone but when he saw Sam he apologized and hung up abruptly. He braced himself expecting the worst news of Mila.

"Come in Sam," Sergeant Rodrick said.

Sam collapsed in a chair and let out all the pent-up pain and uncertainty surrounding his daughters. He explained what his mother told him, and now, his heart was breaking. Sergeant Rodrick sprang into action. He dialed the American Embassy and requested an emergency visa regarding a police matter. It was granted!

Sam and Rachael were at the airport that very

night. They boarded the American Airline for Miami.

Throughout their journey to the airport the couple, who always shared their thoughts, had no words for each other. Apprehension sealed their lips, leaving them with only heavy hearts and thoughts of what ifs. "What if we lose both girls," Rachael thought, but just as quickly as the thought entered her head, she forced it out. She reached for Sam's hand and laced her fingers through his.

At the airport, Sam wrapped his arm around Rachel, kissed her forehead and held her tight as he uttered a little prayer, praying for his beautiful, happy family to be back together again. Tears stung his eyes. He blinked them away.

* * * *

In the meantime, Sofia made a call to Detective Fernandez. He answered right away. She explained the events which led up to Camila's disappearance. Detective Fernandez was shocked. He promised he would be back in town the following day.

The local news reporters had caught wind of the kidnapping and the news was all over the local television. Jane had to move Sofia from her cottage through a back way to her home, just to evade the pesky reporters.

Detective Fernandez called his office to speak to Detective Saunders, but no one knew where he was. Detective Fernandez began to question his judgment of referring Detective Saunders to be the one to take his place on the case of missing Mila. Dark intuitive thoughts were forming in his mind and that was not good.

Erick knew he was becoming a suspect by the minute. He took the steps two at a time as he made his way to his office. Just as he entered the building, he was told Detective Fernandez was awaiting his return call. So instead of making the phone call, Erick did two things. He shredded some papers and threw the rest in his carrying bag. He told himself he had to stay calm.

Erick had a couple of things on his mind! He needed to get to the boatyard as quick as possible, find the girl, kill her and dispose of her body. His chest heaved as his breathing increased with the thought of putting his gun to her head and blowing her brains out.

"Ha, ha, ha," his lips curled up spouting an eerie laugh. "I will cut her down just the way I did that SOB, Sue Ellen."

He hit the highway and drove like the wind.

CHAPTER 28

CHAPTER 28

A gentle moon appeared as if in sympathy of Mila and Camila's plight. About nine feet high, extended on a bed of smaller rocks was a huge gray mesa slab. The girls were puzzled about why the structure was there.

"Why would someone erect this structure and leave it," asked Mila.

"I don't know. Maybe it was a place of worship," Camila answered.

The girls walked around the structure and saw stairs. By the light of the moon and the light from their antique lantern, they carefully climbed to the top of the structure. They decided they would rest there for an hour then move on.

Tucked between large swaths of bark and branches of leaves Mila quickly fell into a fitful asleep. Camila decided she would keep watch as Mila slept.

Camila rubbed her eyes, trying to push the sleep away. She focused on the hunger pangs she felt in her stomach. Her chin slowly sank to her chest. All she remembered was leaning her head back against a cradling rock, looking up at the moon and softly uttering, "Daddy please save us!" Sleep gently wrapped its soothing arms around her and locked her into a quiet slumber.

CHAPTER 29

CHAPTER 29

Julie and Roland found great comfort in playing card games, entertaining friends, watching movies and reading. They tended to stay away from the news because of the crazy politics.

"It is so hypocritical the way these politicians behave Julie, it drives me insane" declared Roland in frustration. He flicked the channels trying to get to Netflix. Suddenly staring right back at him was Hayden, Erick's father! "Julie, come quick!" He shouted.

They both saw the story of Hayden and his wife's death and were left numb with disbelief. Julie dialed her son right away and waited. No answer, it went to voicemail. She chuckled with a slight annoyance and left a message about what she saw on television. After a few moments, she called him right back, thinking maybe this time he would answer.

* * * *

Erick's cell phone on the seat beside him started ringing again. He glanced at it, and saw it was his mother calling and uttered a profanity. "I am not talking to you right now mother dear, I am on a mission," he said softly to himself.

He thought of that night a lot, the night he killed his father. He wanted to do that from the day he made the promise, "you are a dead man."

Suddenly there were flashing lights behind Erick!

"Oh no, not now," he screamed between clenched teeth. I am going too fast." He glanced at the speedometer; he was up there in the 90's. He eased his foot off the gas pedal, allowing his car to reduce its speed. Fortunately for him the highway patrol car with the flashing lights sped past him.

As Erick approached his exit, he noticed some more flashing lights in the distance and a slowing traffic. "This is not good," he thought. He was afraid of being questioned by any cop at the moment. He drove on as the traffic started to pick up.

As the stream of cars moved slowly along the highway, Erick realized it was an accident up ahead. Suddenly there were sounds of sirens everywhere. Cop cars, ambulances, and fire trucks all made their way towards the scene.

A tractor trailer was in the road like a twisted caterpillar blocking Erick's exit. He tried his best to make his way around the accident, but he was prevented by officers on the scene. He wanted so bad to flash his badge and gain access, but he was afraid his cover might be blown.

He slammed back into his car in a rage. He punched his steering wheel, as profanities spilled from his lips. He tried riding on the shoulder of the road and almost got a ticket. Succumbing to defeat, he drove to the nearest motel in the area. His head was pounding. He had to slow his crazy thoughts. He grabbed some dinner, then a sedative. After a piping hot shower, he crawled between the sheets and was out before his head hit the pillow.

* * * *

Back at the precinct, the cops were working overtime trying to piece together Detective Saunders' involvement with Camila's abduction. His shredder was searched, and strips were pasted back together. The contents of his shredder revealed photographs of both girls, also emails from his father, Hayden. They even contacted Julie to verify Saunders' birth name. They also tracked the phone number left by Mila when she called her grandmother.

CHAPTER 30

CHAPTER 30

It was late at night when Sofia and Jane met Sam and Rachael at the airport. Sofia could not contain her composure any longer. The delicate thread held her emotions in check released its hold. Upon seeing Sam, waves of pain and anguish mixed with happiness, yoked her with such a crushing force, she almost fell to the sidewalk. Sam wrapped his arms around his mom and helped her to the car. Sofia and Rachael cried all the way to Sofia's house.

Jane lingered with the family, not wanting to leave them just yet. They decided Sofia should be kept calm so Jane gave her a sedative, encouraged her to take a hot shower and they all tucked her in bed.

Sam and Rachael thanked Jane for being such a strong and caring friend to his mom and begged her to stay the night at Sofia's house. Jane slipped home to grab a few essentials.

Sam was really proud of his mom! He thought she had done very well for herself. His feelings of love and admiration were so overwhelming he quietly entered her room, pulled up an upholstered chair close to her bed, reached out and took her hand and held it for a long time.

He tried to evade the surge of horrific memories, but they came anyway. Dancing behind his closed eyelids, his childhood played out as if in a movie. There was his dad again staring at him with eyes of hate. His snarling lips spouted profane words. Sam thought, "What did we do to make this man hate us so? All we ever wanted was for him to love us."

He thought of his brother and of the space in his heart that would always be empty. Sam tried really hard to resurface from his reverie, but, his weary, conscience was not going to give up so easily. The faces of Mila and Camila bounced into focus, causing his body to convulse. His eyes snapped opened as he uttered sounds of sheer agony.

Rachael was suddenly transfixed. She knew the sounds because she had heard them before. She placed the platter of chicken on the counter and quickly made her way to Sofia's room. The scene she witnessed upon entering the room would be a part of her forever.

Sam's cries of pain woke Sofia. When she opened her eyes and saw Sam's tear streaked face, she cradled him in her arms. Sam was on his knees, with his upper torso wrapped in his mother's arms. She rocked and soothed him and softly sang to him a familiar Spanish song from his childhood.

Just as Jane entered the house, Sofia's phone

rang. It was Detective Fernandez. The detective was very apologetic, blaming himself for the abduction of Camila. He said it was a mistake on his part to let Detective Saunders take the case while he was away.

From the leads obtained by the precinct, it seemed as if Detective Saunders was involved in the abduction of Camila. Detective Fernandez reassured them they are closing in on him and there is a possibility the girls might be ok.

The small group sat silently, prisoners of their own thoughts!

* * * *

On the other side of town, Julie's intuitive mind and her conscience reasoning was hinting disaster! She dialed Erick's number and waited; the phone kept ringing. She left another message!

Roland looked up at his wife and was puzzled to see her distressed expression. "What's wrong?" he asked. Julie explained about the phone calls she made and the messages she'd left for Erick. Roland sighed, leaned back and laced his hands behind his head, giving Julie his full attention.

"Ro, I think Erick is involved in something

sinister. Someone called with a Florida number to verify his birth name," said Julie.

Roland said, "Did you ask who it was?"

Julie said, "Yes, it was a female and she told me she was checking on some of his personal documents. Seeing he had a name change I just assumed everything was legitimate."

Roland said, "Ok, this is what I will do to make sure he is not avoiding you; I will call him tomorrow from the new landline we installed in the office."

Julie said, "Ok baby! Let's call it a night!"

* * * *

The next morning, Erick rolled over, looked at his watch and muttered discontent under his breath. He checked his cell. His mother had left him another message. He responded. "Hi mom, sorry I missed your calls, I am busy at the moment, will call you back later." He dropped his phone next to his gun and got dressed in a hurry.

CHAPTER 31

CHAPTER 31

Pedro was left in charge of the boatyard. He awoke from his tiny cot, thinking of the great night he had last night. When he and the other employees heard the entrance was blocked by the accident, they knew the "boss man" was not coming. So they brought a few of the girls from the boat, got some beers and music and had themselves a wild party.

Pedro slowly walked to Camila's hut and removed the padlock from the hasp. He kicked the door open shouting, "Hey, get up!" Nothing happened, so he moved closer to the cot and kicked the frame. There was still no response, so he reached down and snatched the filthy rags off the bed. The girl was gone! Alarm turned into shock and shock transcended into fear. All Pedro could think about was what had happened to Isabella.

Meanwhile, Detective Fernandez arrived at his precinct very early. He quickly mobilized a SWAT team to undertake the rescue of the young girls who were held in a human trafficking ring. They were able to locate the exact spot through the phone Mila had left for them to track.

* * * *

The boatyard was quiet except for Pedro's kicks and a muffled scream from one of the two boats. The day started like usual but suddenly there was pandemonium! Two large helicopters swooped down unto a clearing near the back perimeter of the compound unloading about sixteen SWAT officers who quickly surrounded the entire area. Loud speakers barked instructions to all. The captain of one boat called the other captain yelling, "Get out, we are surrounded!"

The prisoners exploded onto the deck, screaming, shouting wailing as they jumped off the boats and clambered up the side of the dock. Most of the girls were scantily dressed, some not at all. The officers were taken by surprise! They never expected so many girls to be held on these boats. Disoriented, some of the girls ran to the bushes to take cover. Most of the girls spoke Spanish and some limited English. Detective Fernandez shook his head. This was not what he was expecting. He sprang into swift action.

CHAPTER 32

CHAPTER 32

As Erick neared his exit, he was happy to see the tractor trailer was gone and the coast was clear. He drew nearer and became a bit disconcerted because he thought he heard the hum of a helicopter. He decided to proceed with caution.

Erick slowed his car to a crawl as he pulled into a secondary road leading to the boatyard but from a different direction. Sure enough, he glimpsed a helicopter in the clearing almost at the same spot where he had shot Isabella. His heart pounded against his chest; he was in a panic! "How did this happen?" he questioned himself. Suddenly his phone lit up, it was a text message from Detective Fernandez. "WE WILL GET YOU!" Erick threw the phone through the window as if it were red hot. How he wanted to rip out his steering wheel and toss it, he grabbed his rear-view mirror and was about to yank it when he stopped. His head was pounding, he had to slow down. He reached for his pills popped two in his mouth and swallowed. He quietly got out of his car found his phone and buried it. The paramount thought in his mind was to get to hell out of this place and to get out fast!

CHAPTER 33

CHAPTER 33

Mila and Camila were startled from their sleep and were suddenly alerted for danger. The sun was shining brightly, flooding their high perch with daylight. Something woke them up! They quickly composed themselves and prepared for a quick departure.

Mila looked at the lamp, "Hey the lamp oil is all gone Camila!" Just then a big bird flew over them making a deep clucking sound. The girls dropped to the ground in unison.

Camila said, "That is what woke us up Mila!"

The girls were aware of their thirst and hunger as they made their way down towards the understory.

Mila and Camila pace had slowed. These young girls were thirsty, hungry, tired and frustrated. They had fallen down; their clothes were tattered, and they had bruises and insect bites. Mila walked with a limp and Camila's right arm was in a make shift sling from her shirt sleeve. They decided to find food and fresh water to drink.

Camila put an arm around her sister's shoulder and said to her, "You remember when we were in the Girls Scouts and they told us to eat only fruits that the animals ate, remember?"

"Yes, I do!"

Their prior scouting lessons paid off, because as they came to the edge of the forest, they heard running water and to the far left they noticed a flock of black birds feasting on some kind of fruit.

They approached the tree carefully fearing that they might encounter other dangerous animals in the area. Suddenly Mila stopped, tilted her head backwards and sniffed the air then said "mangoes, Camila, it is a mango tree!"

The girls had a feast, and then they picked up as many mangoes they could carry, tied them up in Mila's shirt and walked towards the sound of the rushing water.

The girls could feel the energy slowly flowing into their veins as they make their way along the water's edge of a brisk river that appears to meander down a progressively sloping hill. Some trees hung their branches so close to the water as it they were washing their leaves. At a certain point of the river there was a blue-green water fall pounding the rocks below sending foamy sprays to the river bank. It was an amazing sight! They were happy to be distracted by this and not dwell on the idea of spending another night in this dense vegetation.

They had walked about a mile and a half when they felt as if they were being followed. They discussed their thoughts and decided to move as quietly as they could. Sure enough, they heard branches and twigs snapping in the distance. Fear mounted.

"We must get to safety Camila!" Mila said between clenched teeth. They moved along the narrow animal path, sometimes running and jumping over small rocks. They were suddenly forced to make a drastic decision because not far behind was a fierce, overgrown, orange cat. It was a bobcat!

A few yards ahead a large tree stump jutted a couple of yards over the water's edge. The girls clambered up the trunk hoping they would not be followed. They were wrong, the cat followed. His piercing sea green eyes held theirs in a determined stare. Camila threw her mangoes at him, she missed. They cat took its time as it approached them. They yelled and shook the stump. The cat stopped and just stared. Mila and Camila were gripped in a paralyzing fear because down below were sharp rocks piercing the rushing water. The animal slowly contracted its body in a pouncing stance. The girls screamed holding unto each other.

Suddenly there was a cracking sound the animal froze in mid-air. Camila and Mila were airborne then crashed to the water!

CHAPTER 34

CHAPTER 34

The case of human trafficking was busted wide open! Television and radio personnel were on the scene. Sirens blared as many ambulances sped through the trees onto the dirt road to the active location.

Detective Fernandez anxiously examined every girl's face in search for Mila and Camila but to no avail! He called Sofia for more information as to where the girls were headed. Sofia had written Mila's direction on her kitchen note pad. She reached for it and read "we will be heading west to the bushes."

"Thanks Sofia" he said.

"Is there any news yet about my granddaughters, detective? She asked.

He said, "Well we found hundreds of girls and they are all alive! I will dispatch a search and rescue team towards the location you gave me. Hang in there! We are not leaving any stone unturned."

"Thanks detective, we do appreciate it," Sofia said.

Detective Fernandez pocketed his cell phone

just as an excited shout came from one of the officers.

"Over here sir!" he yelled

Wedged up between two saplings and covered with leaves was Detective Saunders' car.

"He cannot be very far" one officer said.

"Let's get the dogs!" exclaimed Detective Fernandez.

The captains of the boats were caught and arrested. Two buses filled with girls were sent to the local hospital while the ones with the most severe injuries were placed in the ambulances. The conditions of the girls were unbelievable. Their ages ranged from 12-35. The stories they told through the Spanish translators were horrific. Their bodies showed evidence of lashes, chain marks around ankles and wrists while some bore these marks around their necks.

Reporting the conditions of these young girls was very hard even for the most experienced reporters. Most of them broke down in tears.

The small group in Sofia's house was also looking at the breaking news and they too were emotional as their hearts were breaking for the two girls they love so dearly.

Sam felt as if he was climbing out of his body. He felt helpless. He had no more tears; his tears were all dried up. He had no words; he was now speechless. Despite all the atrocious cruelties his father subjected him, his mom and his brother, Simon, to, he never felt pain like this.

Then suddenly, way in the distance, he heard a sweet voice whispering in his ear, he slowly turned his head and it was Rachael, she hugged him and reached out for Sofia. Sofia reached out for Jane's hand and this small group sank to the floor and they all prayed as they had never prayed before.

CHAPTER 35

CHAPTER 35

At the police station, the team was still discovering new evidence. Some of the evidence linked Detective Saunders to the murders of Hayden Schneider and his wife, Sue Ellen.

Julie was already late for work and she was not having a good day. She had spilled coffee on her shirt, and she had to change. A pimple had grown out on the tip of her nose and it could not be covered by makeup. Most of all, Roland had left early without waking her. She plundered through the hall closet looking for her shoes when the doorbell rang.

Detectives from South Carolina were sent to Julie's house to inform her of the situation with Erick and requested her to accompany them to the local station. She did and was shocked to learn Erick might be involved in the death of his father and stepmother.

After hearing everything, Julie walked out of the small office on wobbly legs. She had to get to a bathroom fast! The toast she ate and the coffee she drank were swiftly rising up through her esophagus. Lucky for her, to her right hung a sign reading Ladies Room.

When she finally got herself together, Julie exited the bathroom with painful and slow steps. She left the building. She grabbed the handrails and was suddenly covered in sunshine caused the golden highlights in her hair to sparkle. At that moment she knew she could not move a step further. She sank to the step, curled one arm around a rail support to keep herself from falling. She called Roland!

Roland pulled up at the station in a hurry. He found his wife sitting solemnly in the same position she sunk to 20 minutes ago. He noticed her pale skin and her limp frame and prayed she was not getting sick again. He helped her up and took her to his car.

Roland quickly called the doctor and was told to bring Julie right away. On their way to the doctor, Julie thought of her life. Right there in the car she made a vow to herself from that day forth, she would stop the pain and hurt her ex-husband and son had caused her. Roland loved her, this she knew, so she would devote the rest of her life making him and herself happy. The first thing was to get better!

CHAPTER 36

CHAPTER 36

The girls hit the water and fought hard to maintain control. They were grabbed by the rushing tide that pushed them down river. Camila's mind raced, she knew she was a stronger swimmer and she had to help her sister who was struggling. Camila forced her way towards a slender rock and grabbed onto it. She knew she had to catch her sister here. There was no time for second guessing! She gave her body enough slack to reach as far out as she could to snatch onto Mila. Just as Camila was about to take hold of Mila there was a heavy whirling sound from overhead. Camila glanced up and just as she did, so the water forced her sister away from her. Without hesitating Camila swam after her.

* * * *

Back at the boatyard, two tracking dogs were brought to the scene. The dogs familiarize themselves with Erick's scent from a towel pulled from his overnight bag. Detective Fernandez gave directions to the small crew of cops and they headed to the bushes with the dogs leading the way.

Erick knew the dogs would soon be after him, so he covered his entire body with mud and made his way along the river beds. Erick had a good half hour jump ahead of the team and he was using all his skills to evade his trackers. He knew he was in good shape and he also knew to slow down the dogs he could urinate on different type of trees to create confusion. He did!

As the minutes dragged on, Erick heard the faint sound of barking in the distance. He ploughed through the undergrowth, reassuring himself he would get away, but to where! On his left was the vast expanse of the river which would be impossible to cross by swimming. Miles ahead was a very busy highway and to his right was more thick dense forest and he knew about the oncoming danger behind him. He wrestled with his thoughts as to what his next move should be.

Erick decided to stay close to the water but keeping a good distance inwards to give himself cover. As he trekked on, he reflected on his life. Did his actions worth this outcome? Hayden was beginning to reach out to him, and the young girls had done nothing to him! Suddenly, he dismissed those thoughts and snapped back to focusing on his present dilemma! The barking dogs were quickly advancing.

Erick suddenly stopped and faded behind a slash pine tree. He remained quiet listening!

Two teenage boys were casting their fishing lines in the water. "We will see who will catch the first trout." One told the other.

"We'll see!" said the other laughing and positioning himself to toss his line.

"Hey Josh, don't forget we promised Ms. Richwood some of our catch for using her boat."

The teenagers popped opened some sodas and made themselves comfortable for a great day of fishing, but this was not going to be a great day for these kids!

Erick appeared; gun drawn as he slowly approached. The boys were terrified, one opened his mouth to speak and Erick motioned for him to be quiet!

As Erick got closer, he pointed to the motor boat pulled onto the bank. "How much gas is in that thing!" he asked softly.

"A-a-a lot," one kid stuttered.

CHAPTER 37

CHAPTER 37

Back at Sofia's house, the telephone rang. Jane was the first one up. She handed it to Sam! Even before Sam could say hello, Detective Fernandez was saying in his ear. "The girls were found in the river; they were rescued by my men and they are on their way to the hospital." Detective Fernandez's voice was full of emotion when he continued, "they are alive!"

Sam thanked the detective, passed the phone to Sofia and flung his arms around Rachel at the same time shouting, "thank you God! They are alive!"

They ran to the car. Sofia was able to get all the details regarding the hospital's location and quickly coded it into her GPS.

Jane was at the wheel as the small group drove in silence. This silence was suddenly punctured by the ringing of Sam's cell. It was Detective Rodrick making his usual check-in call from Barbados.

"Hi Sam, how are you and Rachael holding up? Have you heard anything yet about the girls?"

"Rodrick, yes, yes they were found!" Sam's voice escalated, full of emotion and excitement.

"Sweet Jesus, thank you!" Rodrick continued,

"Man you don't know how our people here in Barbados adore those girls and are praying for them to get back to Barbados safely. As a matter of fact, the Cathedral Church, here on St. Michaels Row, is open every day for anyone who wants to offer prayers."

Sam explained they were on their way to the hospital to see his daughters and he would let them know how much they are appreciated in Barbados.

Jane pulled into the hospital parking lot. She looked around and thought to herself, "hospital parking lots are always full no matter what time of the day!"

Sam helped his mom out of the car as Rachael and Jane brought up the rear. They were all very nervous. Jane wrapped her arm around Rachael giving her all the physical support she could muster. Surprisingly, Sofia had regained her composure and was beginning to pivot into the role of a nurse. They clambered up the steps, through the door into the waiting room. Sofia made her way to the front desk. She had a brief exchange with the clerk who signaled for an attendant to take them to an elevator at the end of a hall.

Jane wanted to give this family their space so they could reunite with their girls. "What a nightmare for this family to endure," Jane thought as she excused herself by offering to get some flowers for Camila and Mila's room. She promised to be with them shortly. Rachael said, "Don't be long Jane!"

Sam, Rachael and Sofia counted the numbers on the rooms, looking for room number B132.

The trio was greeted by a nurse. She introduced herself as Nurse Gayle and said she was the head nurse for the floor. Nurse Gayle sensed their anxiety and without further ado quickly gave the family a breakdown of the girl's conditions. Mila has a superficial head wound on the left caused when the rapid water forced her up against a sharp rock. She also sustained bruises and lacerations to her shoulder and arms of the same left side of her body. Camila has a sprained right wrist and a dislodged right elbow.

Nurse Gayle quickly concluded, "Over all their condition is fair; except for the dehydration and bug bites. Right now, they are sedated and are expected to be alert within an hour." Nurse Gayle gently opened the door of room B132 and ushered the family in.

The girls were breathing in unison. Camila and Mila's beds were arranged close together. Nurse

Gayle told the family the girls requested the bed positioning because they wanted to keep an eye on each other.

A tiny smile cracked the corners of Sam's lips as he moved to the narrow space between the beds. Chills ran up and down his spine. He was mesmerized and he was at a loss for words. "What do I do?" he thought. He fell to his knees in the space that divided the two beds and spread his arms across both of his children and held them tight. Words could not explain the feelings moving through his body. His heart was overcome with joy because this horrific nightmare was finally over.

Rachael moved over to Mila to adjust her pillow and Sofia inspected the IV drips and read their charts.

Suddenly Camila stirred and muttered something unintelligible. Sam rose and hugged both girls. Tears stung his eyes!

Jane entered with an arm full of gorgeous flowers. Her eyes fanned the room, checking on everyone. Sofia was sitting in a wing back chair next to Mila's bed. Rachael was sitting on Camila's bed and Sam sat on a stool between his girls as he caressed their hands.

"Gracias a Dios, they are safe, and Nurse Gayle is preventing any reporter from getting to this floor," Jane said.

"Great!" declared Sam, "We need some together time."

CHAPTER 38

CHAPTER 38

The experienced tracker dogs quickly reoriented themselves after being delayed by the scent of urine on the trees and had made up ground in a short period of time. The team leaped over broken twigs and dense undergrowth as they followed the dogs to the river bank.

"Where do you think he is heading?" asked one officer.

"This is impossible he cannot swim across this vast river!" said another.

"Maybe he wants to end his life." replied the first officer.

Suddenly the dogs moved away from being directly on the river bank and moved to the adjacent freshly bruised path.

* * * *

Erick's body and hair were caked with dried mud, he sustained cuts and bruises to his hands, arms and face. His cold gray eyes were now bloodshot and danced crazily in his head. He was on the water for about fifteen minutes and was speeding full throttle away from his point of exit. He had taken his last pill. His breathing was beginning to normalize. He tried to push everything out of his mind; Detective Fernandez, the boatyard, the girls on the boats, the twin girls, the boys on the beach, his father and most of all, his mother. He had to get away. He would make it out of the country!

The team that was in hot pursuit of Erick was just delivered a punch in the gut! The officers stared in disbelief at the teenagers who laid on the muddy beach; their bodies covered in blood.

"I am calling for Fernandez to come see this," an officer said.

"Let's get an air bus!" another officer screamed. "They are both alive. It seems as if they were pistol whipped!"

Within a matter of minutes, the section of the river bank where the two boys were found was crawling with cops, medical attendants and the media. Police tracker boats cut through the water at high speeds towards Erick.

Above, Erick heard the uncanny sound of a chopper. Leaping frogmen plunged into the water and surrounded him. Erick tried to stand with his hands raised indicating surrender. The cops closed in. Suddenly Erick started shouting "I am sorry, I surrender!"

A police boat had pulled up alongside Erick. The cops moved in to handcuff him, when, without warning, Erick with one swift movement jumped overboard, slicing the water with one quick movement, disappearing beneath the stolen boat. He was a great swimmer! Before the frogmen could take control of the situation, Erick quickly made his way to the other side of the police boat. With swift precise movements he resurfaced and catapulted into the police boat, surprising the officer with a jab to the head then throwing him overboard. It was mayhem! Erick took off at a high speed, leaving the cops in disbelief.

Detective Fernandez gave the orders to shoot Erick after he received news of the escape. Bullets rained down on the boat as Erick accelerated to maximum speeds.

Orders were barked from loud speakers for Erick to surrender. Erick kept on moving. Other police boats joined the chase.

Erick was beginning to lose control. His breath came in rasps, keeping in rhythm with his wildly beating heart that convulsed in his chest. He was beginning to lose focus. His hands shook dangerously then without any warning he was airborne. The bow of the boat was ripped off when it hit the protruding rock which sat in the middle of the river like an island. Erick was unconscious when he was removed from the water.

He awoke in a small hospital room with two officers at the door. He tried to get up but realized he was handcuffed to the bedrails.

CHAPTER 39

CHAPTER 39

The sisters were now fully recovered after spending three days in the hospital. On the evening of the third day they all left the hospital and headed to Sofia's house under the cover of darkness to elude the reporters.

* * * *

Weeks later, Sofia sat up in bed, laid her head back against the headboard and allowed the feelings of complete happiness to envelope her. It had been a long time since she had experienced this level of happiness. She knew it was Simon, her sweet baby boy she was hugging, as she hugged and squeezed her pillow. She knew he was here with them; sharing their happiness. How she wanted to hold him forever!

The phone rang. It was Detective Fernandez

"Hola," Sofia answered

"Hello, this is Detective Fernandez accepting your dinner invitation for tomorrow night," he said.

"Gracias Senor, I feel blessed," She replied.

"Thank you, I'll see you later," he said as he

hung up.

* * * *

Later that week, Sofia invited Jane over for a visit to celebrate the positive closure of their traumatic experience.

"What a blessing, Sofia!" exclaimed Jane

"What a blessing," repeated Sofia, "Thank God!"

Jane got the glasses and Sofia selected their favorite bottle from the beverage refrigerator. She poured the drinks. They took their glasses and sat quietly for a moment, each cherishing the moment of completeness.

Suddenly Jane said, "I think you have found a special friend in Detective Fernandez."

Sofia's eyes twinkled as she replied, "I think so too!"

* * * *

The entire island of Barbados was brimming with joy over the great news of the twin sisters, but the Parish of St. Michael was ecstatic!

The Duncan family was welcomed back to Barbados with rhapsodic songs and prayers from their local church. They were also greeted with a huge ticker tape parade filling sections of the Grantley Adams Airport. It was breathtaking. Pure white confetti floated from above onto the small family who hugged each other as they moved through the billowing snow storm of paper. Calypso singers sang songs as they paid homage to the little Barbadian angels. Young dancers dressed in Caribbean colors moved to the sweet sound of the steel pan music.

The Duncans were finally home! Upon entering their home, they dropped their bags, formed a circle and in their quiet space they thanked the Lord for bringing them back together again.

* * * *

Roland parked his car and helped Julie out. She got out and looked at the large iron gates and read the word penitentiary. She shuddered and Roland gently squeezed her shoulders in his arm as they walked towards the gates.

ABOUT THE AUTHOR

Jurline Younge attended Rutgers the State  University of New Jersey before moving to Sumter SC. Her passion for writing grew as she completed her master's at Cambridge College in Augusta, GA. During her final years as a Special Education teacher, she set her sights on captivating her readers with a spellbinding debut novel, "Where is Mila?"

www.ingramcontent.com/pod-product-compliance
Lightning Source LLC
Chambersburg PA
CBHW030747110726
47900CB00008B/2487